THE BOBBSEY TWINS
AT WHITESAIL HARBOUR

The Rover zipped around the course

THE BOBBSEY TWINS BOOKS

By Laura Lee Hope

The Bobbsey Twins
at Whitesail
Harbour

By

LAURA LEE HOPE

Published by

WORLD DISTRIBUTORS (MANCHESTER) LIMITED

LONDON – MANCHESTER

ENGLAND

First impression . . .   March 1956
Reprinted   . . . . . December 1957
Reprinted   . . . . . September 1959

CONTENTS

CHAPTER I

GOLDFISH IN TROUBLE

"BERT, wouldn't you love to sail on one of these big clipper ships this summer?" Nan Bobbsey asked her twin brother.

The children were looking at a book which contained beautiful pictures of large, old-fashioned ships.

Bert said he certainly would love to take a trip on a clipper, and added, "The captain must have to work hard managing all those sails."

Under each picture was the name of the ship and the names of the sails. Nan laughed and said, "How could anyone ever remember the names of so many sails?"

The twelve-year-old twins, dark-haired and brown-eyed, were interrupted by loud talking on the other side of the living-room. Their younger sister and brother—twins also, but only six years old and blond—were looking into a goldfish tank which stood on a small table.

"Bread crumbs'll make the fish sick," Flossie declared.

"Well, they have to eat something," Freddie answered, sprinkling some of the crumbs on top of the water. "Their food's all gone."

"Why don't you ask Mother about it?" Nan suggested.

Flossie thought this was a good idea, and ran upstairs to speak to Mrs. Bobbsey. Freddie, meanwhile, continued to drop bread crumbs into the tank. The fish nibbled them hungrily.

The Bobbseys never tired of looking at the pretty goldfish, and Waggo, their fox terrier, liked to watch them swim around, too. Now he came into the room and sat down in front of the aquarium.

A few moments later Flossie returned. "Mother says not to give the fish bread crumbs. She'll buy more food this afternoon."

"Then the fish'll have to get their vitamins some other way," Freddie replied importantly. "Let's move the tank over into the sunshine." The little boy had heard his parents talk about good sunshine vitamins.

Bert and Nan, who were again busy looking at the book of clipper ships, did not notice their blue-eyed brother and sister tugging at the table. Inch by inch it began to move across the rug. Suddenly some of the water spilled out of the tank.

"We'd better be careful," Flossie said, alarmed.

Freddie paid no attention. Instead, he gave the table a hard yank, and the glass tank swayed.

Crash!

The aquarium hit the floor and cracked in half, spilling fish, water, sand, and plants over the living-room rug!

"Ooo-eee!" Flossie cried out.

"Quick!" Nan exclaimed, jumping up and rushing over. "Flossie! Freddie! Get some bowls of water as fast as you can!"

Waggo had leaped away when the accident happened. Now he began to sniff at the goldfish flopping on the floor. Suddenly he scooped one up in his mouth and ran towards the kitchen.

"Drop that!" Bert cried. "Waggo, put that fish down!"

The little dog did not obey. He dashed out to the kitchen, through the open door, and into the back yard, which was wet from an early morning shower. The children ran after him.

When Waggo reached a little puddle in the driveway, he dropped the fish into the water. The Bobbsey twins stood and stared. Then they began to laugh.

"You're a good, bad dog!" Flossie shouted gleefully. "That puddle is just as nice as a bowl of water, little fish."

Flossie's mention of a bowl of water reminded the children of the poor goldfish on the living-room rug. They hurried into the house, and took down four bowls from a kitchen cabinet. Quickly they filled them with water. Then Flossie returned to the yard. The others went to the living-room, where the goldfish lay gasping.

"I can't hold 'em," said Freddie as one fish after another slid through his fingers. "Nan, you pick mine up."

Very gently Nan and Bert lifted the fish from the rug into the bowls. The fish began swimming around instantly, as if they were mighty glad to get back into water.

As soon as the children knew the fish were all right for a while, they began to worry about what they were going to live in. The goldfish certainly could not stay in the kitchen bowls.

The noise and excitement had brought Mrs. Bobbsey downstairs. When she saw what had happened, she asked Bert and Nan to go downtown immediately to buy a new tank and more fish food.

"I'll take Freddie's express wagon, Mother," Bert said. "The tank will be too big and heavy for Nan and me to carry."

After the older twins had left the house, Mrs. Bobbsey told Freddie and Flossie the incident could have been avoided. The children should have known it was not wise to move the tank.

"I'm sorry," Flossie said, tears in her eyes.

"I am, too," Freddie added. "I'll get a mop and clean up the water."

Mrs. Bobbsey smiled at them. "I'm not going to punish you," she said, "but I think you should earn the money to pay for the new tank."

"Will it be an awful, awful lot of money?" Flossie asked, worried.

"No," Mrs. Bobbsey replied, "not a great deal, but I believe it will take some time to do it."

After the twins had mopped the rug, they walked into the back yard. Sitting down on the porch steps, they tried to think out how they were going to earn the money.

"What can we do?" Flossie sighed.

Suddenly Freddie's face lighted up. "I know, and it'll be a lot of fun, too."

"What?" Flossie asked.

Freddie leaned over and whispered to her so that no one else could hear what he was suggesting. She clapped her hands gleefully and said:

"But where are we going to get the money to buy them?"

"Out of our piggy banks," Freddie answered.

The twins jumped up and hurried to their bedrooms. Freddie shared a room with Bert, and Flossie slept with Nan.

On their bureaus each of the small twins had a good-sized piggy bank. They put in money whenever they were able to, and sometimes grown-ups put dimes and nickels and even quarters in for them. The children were allowed to do exactly as they pleased with the money from the bank.

Freddie and Flossie ran to their mother. They asked permission to go downtown, promising to be back before lunchtime. When Mrs. Bobbsey said they might, the children hurried off.

Halfway downtown, Flossie and Freddie met Bert and Nan coming back with the new goldfish tank. It sat squarely in the centre of the express wagon.

"That's better than the old one," Flossie remarked.

"Yes, and it's a little larger," said Nan. "You can help us put the fish in right away."

"But we don't want to go back now," said Freddie.

Bert and Nan looked surprised and asked why not. Flossie and Freddie said they had a secret errand downtown. They would be home after a while. They had just started away, when Bert said:

"Here comes Danny Rugg!"

"Oh, bother!" said Nan.

The Bobbsey twins did not like Danny Rugg. He was a little taller than Bert, though the same age, and he was always playing mean tricks on the children at school.

"What have you got there?" Danny asked, coming across the street. "Hey, it's a new goldfish tank," he said, answering his own question.

The Bobbseys merely said hello, and Bert and Nan started pulling the express wagon along the street. Danny was annoyed that they would not talk to him.

"Say, you two are a couple of sissies," he said. "Not even strong enough to carry that tank. I could carry it alone. I wouldn't need an old express wagon."

Still the Bobbsey twins said nothing to him.

"I could carry that tank on one shoulder," Danny boasted.

With this, he reached down and started to drag the aquarium from the wagon.

"Get away from there, Danny Rugg!" Bert shouted.

"I won't hurt your old tank," Danny said.

He gave Bert a push, and lifted the tank. Bert took it away from him and set it down, then shoved Danny off. The bully shoved back.

Nan decided that the best thing for her to do would be to start home with the wagon while the boys were pushing each other around. She started off at a run, but Danny had another scheme. He ran, too.

The next instant he caught up to her, and gave the wagon a violent kick. It tilted and the tank slid towards the pavement.

CHAPTER II

TWIN SALESMEN

AS the glass goldfish tank toppled towards the ground, Nan grabbed for it from one side and Bert from the other. Together they managed to keep it from hitting the pavement.

"Danny Rugg, I wish you'd move away from this town and never come back!" Bert said angrily. He wanted to fight the other boy, but he had a job to do.

Danny suddenly began to laugh. "I'm going to move away for the summer, and that's more than you're going to do," he said. "I'm going to a boys' camp at Whitesail Harbour. Don't you wish you were going?"

"Not if you're going to be there!" Bert snapped, and walked off. Anyway, he thought, the Bobbseys often went on trips. Ever since the twins were small, their mother and father had taken them many places. They had had exciting holidays at the seaside, a farm, and at camp.

Flossie and Freddie had not seen the trouble with Danny, and walked on until they came to a pet shop. Going inside, Flossie told the owner, Mr. Rodin, that she would like to see some goldfish.

"To put in that tank your brother and sister just bought?" the man asked. "Did those poor fish die?"

Flossie and Freddie told him no, the fish were all right, but Mrs. Bobbsey had said they must earn the money to pay for the new tank. This was what they wanted to do: buy some goldfish from the man and sell them to their friends, so they could earn enough to pay for the new tank.

"That sounds very fine," Mr. Rodin said, smiling.

Flossie told him they had lots of friends. She was sure they would be glad to buy at least one goldfish each.

Mr. Rodin wished the children lots of luck in their little business and said he would make a bargain with them. The twins could buy the fish from him at exactly the price he paid for them, not the higher price he charged other people.

"Why, thank you!" the children said together.

"Now tell me how much you want to spend and I'll see what I can do for you," Mr. Rodin said.

When Flossie and Freddie told him they had thirty-six cents between them, the man led them to a large tank where pure white fish were swimming around. As the sun shone through a window on them, they seemed to have colours like the rainbow.

"They're be-yootiful!" Flossie exclaimed.

Freddie was more interested in the tank of black fish, with tails that swept back and forth. Mr. Rodin said they were called fantails.

"How would it be," he added, "if you take three white ones and three black ones?"

"That would be wonderful," said Flossie. "What can we carry them in?"

Mr. Rodin said he had small cardboard boxes, and he would put one fish in each box. He took six boxes from a shelf and filled them half full of water. Then he took a net and dipped it down into the tanks to catch the fish. Flossie and Freddie were sure Mr. Rodin was picking out the prettiest ones.

After the fish were in the boxes, Mr. Rodin fastened the lids. The twins gave him their money, thanked him, and proudly walked from the store.

"Where shall we go first?" Flossie asked.

Freddie thought a moment, then suggested they go to the Blakes.

"I'm sure my friend Teddy would like a pet."

When they reached his house, the Bobbseys found out from Mrs. Blake that Teddy was not at home.

"Would you like to buy a fish for him?" Freddie asked. Teddy's mother looked surprised, but when the twins explained why they were selling the fish, Mrs. Blake smiled and said she would take a couple.

"I believe I'll buy one white and one black," she said.

They told her that each fish would cost fifteen cents, and she went to get her purse. Returning, she said she would go right downtown and buy a tank and some food for the fish.

"That will give nice Mr. Rodin some more business," Flossie said.

The children decided to go next to a little friend of Flossie's named Susie Larker. She was very excited to hear what Freddie and Flossie were doing, and asked her mother at once if she might buy some fish. Fortunately Mrs. Larker said Susie could have two.

"We're making money fast," said Freddie, as he and Flossie left Susie's home.

But after this, business did not seem to be so good, because at three places where they stopped, the people did not want any fish. The twins decided they had stayed away from home as long as they dared, so they went back, still wanting to keep their work a secret.

"What are we going to do with these two boxes?" Flossie asked.

Freddie was not sure. Then suddenly he had an idea. "We'll hide them on a shelf in the garage, and then go out tomorrow morning and sell the fish," he suggested.

Before supper that evening, Mr. Bobbsey told his children about something which was to take place in the recreation building on the shore of Lake

Metoka. There were to be summer classes for children of Bert and Nan's age.

"I have a circular here telling about it," Mr. Bobbsey said to his older twins. "Why don't you two look it over, and see if you would like to join any of these classes?"

Bert and Nan were interested at once. They carefully read what classes there were to be, and Nan said she would like to join a class in plaited-rug making.

"Here's one that sounds fine," Bert spoke up. "Making model motorboats. At the end of the season, they're going to race the boats on the lake. I'd like to join that class, Dad."

Mr. Bobbsey gave Bert and Nan the money to pay for the classes, and the next morning they hurried off to register.

Reaching the lake, they separated. Nan went to the rug class, while Bert headed for the room where the model motorboats were to be made. A friendly young man walked up to him.

"I'm Harold Warren, your teacher," he said.

Bert was the first one to arrive, but within a few minutes several other boys walked in. Bert noticed a large glass case containing a very fine-looking model motorboat on the teacher's desk. He asked about it.

"It's my own special boat, the *Challenger*," Mr. Warren answered. "It once won the national championship race."

"That's great," Bert said. "Does it still run?"

"Oh, yes," said Mr. Warren.

Bert and several other boys looked at one another, the same idea in their minds. Bert finally spoke for them:

"Mr. Warren, would you let us see the *Challenger* in action?"

The teacher hesitated. He said that he would not dare let the boat run by itself on the lake, because it went so fast that it could easily get out of sight and be lost.

The boys looked disappointed. If the boat could go that fast, they certainly would like to watch it. Seeing the looks on their faces, Mr. Warren said:

"In most midget motorboat racing, we use a pole to which are attached two rods called a bridle and a cable. The boat is fastened to the rods. Then the boat goes round and round the pole and cannot be lost."

He went on to say that they might set up a pole with a bridle and cable in the lake and attach the boat to it.

"I'll put the pole up," Bert offered.

He took off his socks and shoes and rolled up his trousers. Mr. Warren got the pole from a cabinet in the classroom and handed it to Bert. Then they all went out to the lake.

After wading into the water, Bert began hammering the pole down into the sand. When it was firm enough, he came ashore, and Mr. Warren showed him where to fasten the *Challenger* to the bridle and handed it to Bert.

In a few seconds the boat was on its way. How fast the little boat could travel! The *Challenger* went whizzing round and round in a circle.

"Wow! Would I like to own that!" Bert exclaimed.

He had hardly said this when the pole began to loosen. The boat swished around and zigzagged in the water instead of going in a circle.

"Oh!" Bert cried, trying to grab the pole.

The next instant it flew out of the water. The small motorboat sped across the lake, dragging cable and pole with it!

CHAPTER III

A GIFT FOR WAGGO

WITHOUT a moment's hesitation Bert dived into the water. He must stop the *Challenger*!

The boy was making good time after the runaway boat, when suddenly the *Challenger* threw off the bride and cable. After that there was no catching it!

Bert looked up. Seeing the boat getting farther and farther away, he wondered what to do. As he looked around, he saw a motorboat coming across the lake, and frantically waved at it. The boat churned up, alongside of Bert, who pulled himself up over its side. A nice-looking, sun-tanned young man was piloting it.

"Can I help you?" he asked.

"Will you please take me as fast as you can down the lake?" Bert requested. "You see that midget boat getting away? It belongs to Mr. Warren and it's a championship boat. It's worth a lot of money. We mustn't lose it!"

The man was very glad to speed up his own boat and race after the *Challenger*. Bert was sure he would overtake it in a few minutes, but such was not the case. The little boat seemed to be gathering more speed every moment.

"Jiminy, that little boat's like a rocket!" the young man said.

"Oh!" Bert cried suddenly. "There comes another boat and it doesn't see the *Challenger*!"

It appeared certain there was going to be a crash! Bert was so excited he jumped up and down, yelling to the driver of the other boat. Evidently his voice did not carry that far, because the pilot paid no attention to him.

"What'll we do?" Bert worried. "If the *Challenger* is ruined, I never can face Mr. Warren."

His own pilot, seeing that an accident was near, blew his horn. The driver of the other boat turned his head. Bert pointed to the midget motorboat. This time the man saw it, and swerved out of the way, just missing the *Challenger*.

"Grab that boat!" Bert cried. "It's running away and it's valuable!"

The driver put on a burst of speed and came alongside the speeding *Challenger*. Quickly he threw water on to make its engine stop. Then he reached down and grabbed hold of it. The valuable midget speedboat had been rescued!

"Well, I'm very glad I was able to save it for you," the man said. "If that little boat is ever in a race, I'd like to see it. I bet it would beat all the others."

Bert's driver asked where the boy wanted to be taken, and Bert told him that he was attending Mr. Warren's class. The man headed back in that direction. Bert thanked him and waded ashore with the *Challenger*.

The excitement of the runaway boat had brought all the children from their classrooms. Now they stood on the shore, cheering Bert for his rescue. Among them was Nan. She gave her brother a big hug, embarrassing him very much.

"Aw, I didn't do anything," he said.

"That's right, you didn't," said a voice which he recognized as that of Danny Rugg.

Bert paid no attention, but he wondered why Danny was there.

Bert went on, "The two men in the big boats were the ones who really rescued the *Challenger*, Mr. Warren," he said, handing over the valuable midget boat. "I'm certainly glad nothing happened to it."

The teacher smiled. "Accidents will happen," he said, "but I admit I'm mighty glad to have my boat back."

He walked to the classroom, placed the *Challenger* back in its glass case and locked it.

The class was nearly over, but Bert and the other boys planned to report at nine o'clock the next morning. As Bert walked away he met Nan, and the two strolled home together.

"What did you do in your class?" Bert asked his sister.

"Our teacher—her name is Mrs. Shole—gave us a lecture on plaited-rug making. I'm sure it's going to be lots of fun. Now we have to bring yarn, wool, and rags to class to make ropes of them."

"You can have my green shirt that I spilled ink on in school." Bert laughed. "And that red sock—you know the one I mean. Waggo chewed up the mate to it."

When they reached home, Nan went at once to find her mother and ask what other bits of cloth she might take. Mrs. Bobbsey suggested that Nan look in the family rag bag. The little girl was puzzled. Laughingly, her mother said:

"When I was a girl, every bit of old cloth in our house was put into a great big bag and hung in a cupboard. Whenever anyone needed a rag, he always went to the rag bag."

"I've never seen one around our house," Nan said.

"No, you never have. But we have a big rag box in the attic. I'll go up with you and see what we can find."

They climbed to the attic and examined all the things in the box. Finally Nan selected part of an old blue wool dress, and half a torn scarf.

Going back to the second floor, she found the sock and shirt which Bert had mentioned.

Flossie came running into the room and wanted

to hear all about Nan had done in her class. Hearing that her sister was looking for wool, Flossie offered a pink jersey which had a long rip in the sleeve.

"Please take this, Nan," she said. "I think pink will look awfully pretty in a rug, don't you?"

Nan thought indeed it would. The more colours she could have, the prettier the rug would be. She found a light blue blouse of her own which was too small. Taking the two articles with her, she went to ask her mother if she might use them. Mrs. Bobbsey agreed.

The next morning Nan left the house early with her various pieces of wool. When she reached her class Mrs. Shole was already there. The teacher said she thought Nan's wool would make a very pretty rug.

"What we are going to do first," Mrs. Shole said, "is to make a small practice rug. If it turns out well, then I'm going to suggest we make larger rugs as birthday gifts for people in our families."

"Our cook Dinah is having a birthday in a couple of weeks," Nan said. "I'll make one for her. And my practice rug, how big will that be, Mrs. Shole?"

The teacher said it would be about twelve inches by eighteen inches.

"That will just be big enough for our dog's indoor basket." Nan laughed. "I think Waggo needs a new rug."

As soon as all the pupils assembled, Mrs. Shole told them to cut their wool into strips. Each one was to be about three-quarters of an inch wide and fifteen inches long. After the girls had done this, she told them to sew the long edges of each strip together. When this was finished, they were to turn each strip right side out.

"How in the world can you do that?" a girl sitting next to Nan asked.

Nan could not answer the question, but in a few minutes the teacher did. She brought each girl a stout safety pin, told her to put it into the end of the strip, then pull the strip over it. In a moment each girl had the strips right side out.

"When any of you have three strips ready, come up here to the front of the class and start plaiting them," Mrs. Shole said.

Nan, who had always loved to plait hair ever since she was a little girl, was the first one to reach the front of the room. The teacher told her first to sew the ends of the three strips together. Then she was to attach this with a pin to a board which had been put up along one side of the schoolroom.

"Now start your plaiting," Mrs. Shole said.

Nan plaited very quickly. Then she went back to her seat and started three more strips.

The other girls were working quickly, too. They decided to have a race to see which one would finish her practice rug first.

It was not possible to complete any that day because the bell rang and class was dismissed. But Nan came early the next morning, and started work before many girls had come.

When the pupils had several plaits ready, their teacher showed them how to place the plaits on a table in a circle and sew the coils together. Little by little the rugs grew, and by the end of the period, Nan's rug was finished.

"May I take it home today?" she asked the teacher. "I'd love to give it to Waggo to sleep on tonight."

"Yes indeed," Mrs. Shole said, laughing. "But I think it's almost too pretty for a dog to lie on."

Nan smiled, too. But she could not agree with what the teacher had said. Waggo was one of the very nicest dogs in Lakeport, and she was sure he would keep the rug clean.

Nan ran most of the way home. Reaching the house, she hurried into the back yard and went to the kennel where Waggo stayed in the daytime. He was not there. Not seeing him around, Nan walked back to the kitchen and asked the kindly Negro cook Dinah where the dog was.

"Waggo?" Dinah asked. "I haven't seen that dog all morning."

"You mean he didn't eat breakfast?"

Dinah shook her head. "To tell you the truth, Nan, Waggo wasn't in his basket when I came downstairs early this mornin'."

"You mean Waggo may be lost?" Nan asked in alarm.

CHAPTER IV

A FUNNY MISTAKE

"DINAH, it would be dreadful if something has happened to Waggo!" Nan cried.

"Indeed it would," Dinah agreed. "I never thought about that. But you know that dog is very smart. He always seems to know how to take care of himself."

Just the same, Nan was worried. Flossie, coming into the kitchen, heard what had happened.

"Let's go and hunt for Waggo!" she cried, dashing out of the back door.

By this time Bert and Freddie also came into the kitchen and heard that Waggo was gone. Freddie said he had seen the dog heading for the stream at the back of their garden.

"I thought he was going for a little swim, b-but maybe he got in trouble!"

Since it was now half-past twelve, it seemed likely that their pet might indeed be in trouble.

The four twins hurried towards the river. Bert whistled for Waggo as they went.

But the dog did not come, and the children became more and more alarmed.

Finally they reached the stream and looked up and down. Each child had the same dreadful thought in his mind. Suppose poor Waggo had drowned! None of them dared say so aloud. It was too sad a thought.

In a few moments Flossie began to cry, and tears came to Freddie's eyes, too. Bert and Nan comforted them, saying that Waggo would surely turn up.

"He may just have gone to play with some other dogs," Bert suggested.

Nan decided to walk along the river and keep on calling. At the same time she looked for tiny footprints. Soon she saw some.

Nan called to the others and quickly they followed the small prints.

"Waggo! Here, Waggo!" Freddie called, and Bert whistled once more.

Suddenly they heard barking. There was no mistaking that shrill bark. It was Waggo!

"There he is! I see him!" Freddie shouted.

"Where?" Flossie asked.

"Inside that boathouse over there," Freddie pointed.

Waggo was jumping against the door of the boathouse. He was barking joyfully now, and wagging his tail.

Of course Waggo could not say why he was a prisoner in the boathouse, but Bert guessed that he had pushed the door open to get in and then had not been able to get out.

By now Freddie had run to the door and opened it. Waggo leaped out and licked the little boy's face so hard it tickled him and made him laugh. Then Waggo tried to thank the other Bobbseys by licking their hands and faces, and jumping around in circles, barking.

"You must be awfully hungry," Flossie said, petting the dog. "We'll go right home and give you breakfast and lunch."

Waggo did not wait for a second invitation. He bounded ahead of the children. Though they all ran fast, Waggo reached the house first and barked at the kitchen door.

"Well, I declare to goodness," said Dinah. "You're home again, Waggo."

She opened the door for him, and, being a very wise person, she knew at once he was asking for food.

Before she served lunch to any of the Bobbsey family, Dinah prepared a big bowl of food for Waggo. He gobbled it very quickly, and then came and licked her hand in thanks.

Mr. Bobbsey arrived for lunch, and Bert talked to him about the midget speedboat he was making in Mr. Warren's class.

"When I get the wooden part all made, Dad," Bert said, "I'd like to buy a motor to put in it."

His father smiled. "Well, I suppose a motorboat isn't much good without a motor. But you know, Bert, engines for those little speedboats are pretty expensive."

Bert said he knew they were. The cheapest one cost twelve dollars, and the one which Mr. Warren had in his *Challenger* must have cost at least fifty dollars.

Mr. Bobbsey thought a few minutes. Then he said, "Don't you think you should wait until you see what kind of a boat you make? After all, it might not be worth an expensive motor."

"It's going to be a good boat, Dad," Bert replied.

"If you make a very good one that warrants a motor," his father promised, "I'll pay part of the cost, providing you earn the rest."

"How much would you give me towards it, Dad?" Bert asked. "I only have fifty cents in my bank."

"Four or five dollars," Mr. Bobbsey replied.

This meant Bert would have to earn about six or seven dollars himself. He knew that when he worked down at his dad's lumber-yard, it took a long time to make that much.

After lunch Bert called on his friend Charlie Mason. Charlie was also in the boat-making class and had spoken to his parents about a motor. Mr. Mason had told Charlie about the same as Mr. Bobbsey had told Bert.

"Do you suppose we could make a motor?" Bert suggested.

"That's an idea. Let's try it," Charlie answered.
He said there was an old vacuum cleaner in their cellar which did not work any more. Perhaps his mother would let him take the motor out of it. Bert knew there was a broken electric fan in the Bobbsey attic. He would ask his mother for it.

It was not long before the boys had the old, broken gadgets in the workshop over the Bobbsey garage. They bolted the door so that no one could come in and make fun of what they were doing. They took a wire and attached it to a long, round metal pin. Next they took two gears, one from the vacuum and the other from the electric fan, and fitted them together.

Bert then took the rod and pushed it through a hole in the centre of the gear. The two boys worked hard for a long while, then Bert said:

"What say we try it now, Charlie?"

"Okay."

Charlie picked up one end of the wire and attached a plug to it. Proudly he pushed the plug into a socket. Bert clicked on a switch to the motor, and the boys waited to see the gears go round and round.

But nothing happened.

Looking through the keyhole of the door was little Freddie Bobbsey. He had followed the boys to see what they were doing. Finding the door locked, he had decided to peek at them anyway. Now he heard Bert say:

"Charlie, I guess we'll have to give up. We don't

know enough about motors to put one together ourselves."

"I'm afraid you're right," Charlie agreed.

Freddie skipped down the steps and ran to find Flossie. She was playing with a doll in the back yard.

"Flossie," Freddie said excitedly, "Bert and Charlie can't make their motor work. If Bert can't earn enough money he won't have a motor for his new speedboat!"

"I know what let's do," Flossie said. "Why can't you and I sell twice as many goldfish and give half the money to Bert?"

Since they had sold six fish in three days, Freddie thought this was a very good idea. He suggested they start off at once and go to the pet shop to buy more fish. Running into the kitchen, he told Dinah that he and Flossie were going downtown on a little errand.

Bert and Charlie, meanwhile, had left the garage. Flossie ran and climbed up to a shelf where she and Freddie kept the money they were making for the goldfish tank. She emptied the little box and put the money into her pocket.

Then she met Freddie and the two children went off down the street. Freddie told Flossie that Dinah had asked him to stop at the fish market on his way back and bring home a quart of oysters because Mr. and Mrs. Bobbsey were having guests for dinner. Dinah wanted to make a very special dish with oysters.

"We'd better go to the fish market first, so we won't forget our errand," Flossie giggled.

When the children came to the market they bought the oysters, which the man put in the same kind of carton as was used for the goldfish.

"We'd better not try to sell oysters by mistake," Freddie grinned as they left the market and entered the pet shop.

Since the small twins were regular customers of Mr. Rodin's, he waited on them at once, putting four black and four white goldfish into a box which was exactly the same size as the one the oysters were in. He said he was sorry he had no more small boxes to put the individual fish in.

"I'll lend you a little net to take the fish out," he said. "I think it will fit in your pocket, Freddie."

Freddie took the net, and the children went off down the street. On the way Flossie suddenly spied the big clock which was in the tower of the town hall.

"My goodness, Freddie," she said, "it's almost supper-time. I remember now, Mother said you and I and Bert and Nan have to eat early. I guess it's because company is coming."

"If we can't sell the fish now, we'll have to hide them," Freddie said.

When they got home Flossie put the box up on the shelf, while Freddie went into the house and set the box of oysters in the pantry. Dinah thanked him, and said she was glad he had not forgotten to do the errand.

The four Bobbsey twins were served an early supper, and then they went to their rooms to play. Presently Freddie and Flossie were told it was bedtime, and soon both of them were sound asleep.

After a while it seemed to Freddie that something very strange was happening. Somebody was pulling at him, trying to waken him. Finally he heard a far-away voice say:

"Freddie, wake up! We can't eat goldfish for supper."

CHAPTER V

AN ANNOYING BOY

"I DIDN'T eat goldfish for supper!" Freddie replied sleepily.

"I know you didn't," said his father, who was trying to prop Freddie up in bed and arouse him enough to learn what had happened.

Freddie fell back on the pillow. His father sighed, deciding it was no use. Freddie was too sleepy to talk intelligently.

"I'll try Flossie," he told himself, and tucked Freddie back under the covers.

Going to the next room, he roused his little daughter. Sleepy-eyed, she looked at her father and yawned.

"Is it morning already?" she asked.

"No, dear, it's not morning yet," Mr. Bobbsey said, and added laughing, "Listen, Flossie, your mother and I and our guests want to eat oysters, not goldfish."

"Goldfish?" Flossie repeated, her eyes growing very large. "No, no, you mustn't eat my goldfish."

Mr. Bobbsey was mystified. "*Your* goldfish? Now look, Flossie, where are the oysters you were supposed to buy? Dinah wants to know."

"In the pantry, Daddy."

"But they're not," Mr. Bobbsey said. "We found a white box, but it was full of goldfish. What happened?"

Suddenly Flossie laughed. "I guess Freddie and I made a mistake." She leaned very close to Mr. Bobbsey. "Daddy, can you keep a big, big secret?"

"I certainly can," he assured her.

Flossie whispered that she and Freddie were in the goldfish business to pay for the new aquarium and to help Bert buy a motor.

"Well, that is certainly very fine," Mr. Bobbsey said, "and you may be sure I'll keep your secret. How are you and Freddie making out in your business?"

Flossie told him proudly that they were doing very well. They had sold goldfish to nearly all their friends, and every one of those friends had promised to keep their secret.

"Well, now, my dear," her father said, "how about telling me where the oysters are?"

"I guess they must be on the shelf in the garage," Flossie giggled.

They had a good laugh about the mix-up, and Mr. Bobbsey promised that he would exchange the two boxes. Only he and Dinah would know the secret. The little girl lay down again. He kissed her, pulled up the light blanket, and closed the door.

Next morning both Flossie and Freddie wondered if they had dreamed the whole thing. But after they had had breakfast, the small twins went outside to talk to each other about it.

It was true! When no one else was around they went in and spoke to Dinah. She laughed heartily, and said yes, when she had gone into the pantry to get the box of oysters, what did she see inside but goldfish swimming around!

The children started off early and had very good luck. They sold goldfish at the first two houses they tried. They kept to their rule of going only where they knew the people. As the twins came down the steps of the second house, who should be coming along the street but Danny Rugg!

"What have you got there?" he called.

"Goldfish," Flossie replied.

"Are you still working on goldfish and goldfish tanks?" Danny sneered. "You're a couple of silly kids."

With that he yanked the box out of Freddie's hand and opened it to look at the fish. He put his hand down inside.

"Don't you dare hurt our fish!" Flossie screamed.

She pulled the box from his hand and started to run, but the water splashed out, and she stopped.

Freddie had an idea. "Flossie," he called, "go to the next house, the Johnsons'. I'll take care of Danny."

The little fellow grabbed the older boy's coat and held on to it. Danny squirmed and tried to get out of Freddie's grasp, but by the time he jerked free, Flossie had climbed the steps of the porch and rung the bell. Mrs. Johnson opened the door almost immediately.

Danny was forced to stop annoying Freddie, who said to him, "I thought you were going to camp."

"I am," Danny answered. "Tomorrow."

"You can't go too soon to suit the Bobbseys," Freddie said stoutly.

"What makes you think I want to stay around here anyhow?" Danny replied. "You ought to see Whitesail Harbour. It's a grand place. There's a big bay with lots of sailing boats on it. And my camp is right along the shore. We go swimming four times a day."

"It does sound nice," Freddie conceded. "But it's nice in Lakeport, too. We have a lake here."

Danny said Lake Metoka was just a little tiny thing compared to Whitesail Harbour. And it only had small motorboats on it, too. Whitesail Harbour had great big ships.

At this moment Mrs. Johnson came down the steps with Flossie. She had seen Danny bothering the twins even before Flossie rang the bell, and had decided to speak to him. When Danny realized this, he ran off down the street.

"Was that Danny Rugg?" Mrs. Johnson asked. "He's such a mean boy."

The small Bobbsey twins agreed and thanked her for getting rid of him. After she had bought a black and a white goldfish, the children went on to look for another customer.

While the small twins were busy, Bert and Nan were working hard in their classes. Nan had already started her large plaited rug, and Bert had almost finished the hull of his midget motorboat. Just before the class ended, Mr. Warren gathered the boys around him.

"I want to tell you that when this course is ended," he said, "there will be an exhibition of all boats, and a race among those which have motors."

"I'll never finish in time," Charlie Mason wailed.

Mr. Warren said he would be glad to give the boys extra help outside class, or they could take their boats home to work on.

"I want to get in the race!" cried several of the boys, including Bert.

"There's to be an even bigger race on Lake Metoka," Mr. Warren said, "and the winner in our group will be allowed to enter it."

He explained that the race was open to anyone in the county who had already won some smaller race.

"I'm going to work very hard and try to get my boat into our class race," Bert told himself.

He would work in his father's lumber-yard every afternoon, and on Saturdays when the class did not meet he would spend the whole day there.

"I suppose it is too much to hope for," Mr. Warren went on, "but I should tell you boys that the winner of the county race on Lake Metoka will be entitled to enter the big Interstate Race at Whitesail Harbour."

Whitesail Harbour! Bert instantly remembered that Danny Rugg was going there. On the way home he kept thinking how lucky Danny was to be able to spend time at a camp on Whitesail Harbour. No doubt Danny would see the interesting motorboat race.

As Bert walked along the street, with his nearly completed boat under his arm, Freddie and Flossie ran up to him. They had finished selling their fish and were on their way home.

"Is this your boat?" Freddie asked. "It looks super!"

"Do you think so?" Bert asked, his eyes shining.

"Yes, I do," his small brother answered. "I don't care what Danny says about all the big boats on Whitesail Harbour. I think little tiny boats are better anyhow."

Bert told the twins what Mr. Warren had said about the interstate racing at Whitesail Harbour and added:

"I'd love to go, but I guess there's no chance of that. What else did Danny say about Whitesail Harbour?"

When Freddie told him, Bert wished all the more that he might be going there. Then suddenly he realized that first of all he must prove to his father that the little boat under his arm was good enough to have a motor installed in it.

As Bert turned into the walk leading to the Bobbsey house, he wondered if his dad would be home to lunch. And if he were, what would his decision be?

CHAPTER VI

FREDDIE IN MISCHIEF

MR. BOBBSEY took Bert's boat and looked it over carefully. He did not say anything for several seconds, as he felt the wood, peered inside the midget speedboat, and then examined the bottom where the keel was.

"Well, Bert, for a beginner I should say you have done an excellent job."

"Thank you, Dad," Bert replied. "Do you think it would be all right for me to buy the motor?"

Putting one hand on Bert's shoulder, Mr. Bobbsey told his son that he wanted him to have a motor very much, but he thought the boat needed some improvements before it would be ready for a motor.

"I don't know how much money you've earned so far," his father said. "How much is it?"

Bert thought for a few seconds, then said he had two dollars. He still had several days in which to work, and he hoped to get the full amount by that time.

"The only trouble," Bert said, "is that it takes time to put the motor in the boat, and after that, I have to practice. If it takes too long, I'll miss my chance."

When Mr. Bobbsey saw the worried look on Bert's face, he said, "I'll tell you how I can help you. I'll raise your pay at the lumber-yard."

Bert was very happy to hear this, and promised to work even harder in return for the extra money. Freddie and Flossie had been listening, but not saying a word. As soon as lunch was over, they found Dinah and her husband Sam in the kitchen. Sam was a smiling, white-haired man who helped Mr. Bobbsey in the lumber-yard.

"Sam, can you help us with some 'rithmetic?" Flossie asked.

The man scratched his head, saying he would do the best he could. Really, Dinah was better at arithmetic than he was.

"What is it you all want to know?" Dinah asked, looking up from a bowl in which she was mixing a cake.

"Somehow we have to get up to twelve dollars or maybe more," Flossie said.

"Why do you have to do that?" Sam asked.

Flossie said that if Sam would promise to keep a secret, she would tell him why. He grinned and promised. So Flossie told him about wanting to help Bert get the motor for his motorboat, and Freddie said:

"We paid for the new goldfish tank. And we made one dollar for Bert."

"Why, that's splendid!" Sam exclaimed. "You mean you earned all that sellin' goldfish?"

The small twins nodded. Then Freddie said he wanted to know how much Bert had earned and how much money he was going to make during the next few days. Sam said he could only guess at this, but it would not be more than three dollars.

"Then how much are three dollars and one dollar and five cents and three pennies and ten cents?" Flossie asked.

"Now let me see, honey child," Dinah said, putting down her spoon. She began to count on her fingers. Sam laughed and said the answer was four dollars and eighteen cents.

"Now, tell me," said Freddie, "how much is four dollars and eighteen cents and four or five dollars?"

Sam and Dinah both laughed. They said what did Freddie mean four or five dollars? Freddie remembered his father telling Bert he would give him four or five dollars. So Freddie did not know which it was to be.

"Are you sure this motor is only twelve dollars?" Sam asked Freddie.

The little boy thought this was right, but he was becoming more confused every minute. He was not really sure of anything, except that somehow he and Flossie would have to make still more money selling goldfish to help Bert get the motor. Suddenly Freddie had an idea.

"Flossie, let's go down and ask Bert's teacher about the motor."

"But if we do that, Bert will know our secret," Flossie objected.

"Then let's go just when the class is over," Freddie said.

Next morning the small twins watched the clock. When they thought they could reach Bert's classroom before the teacher had left, they started off. It was a long walk, and they began to worry about whether they would be too late. But they reached the room just as Mr. Warren was locking the door.

"Is your name Mr. Warren?" Flossie asked him.

The man smiled, saying it was. What could he do for them?

"We're Bert Bobbsey's brother and sister," Freddie spoke up manfully. "We want to know how much a motor will cost to go into Bert's boat."

Mr. Warren said that for the type of boat Bert had made, he should have one that cost no less than twelve dollars. Hearing this, the small twins sighed deeply.

"Then I'm afraid," Flossie spoke up, her big, blue eyes looking straight at the teacher, "that there aren't that many goldfish in Lakeport."

Mr. Warren looked so surprised that Flossie knew she must have said something strange. So she explained just what she and Freddie were trying to do.

When he heard this, Mr. Warren laughed a very jolly laugh, and he said he thought it was wonderful for Bert's brother and sister to do this. He ended by saying:

"I'd like to help you. I think Bert's boat is going to be a dandy one and he should have a motor in it. I can buy motors wholesale, and I believe I can get you a twelve-dollar one for ten dollars. Would that help you?"

"Oh, yes," they cried together.

Flossie jumped up and down, clapping her hands. Freddie gave a sound something like an Indian war-whoop and ran round and round in a big circle three times.

"But you'll keep our secret, won't you?" Flossie asked Mr. Warren.

"Indeed I will," he promised.

The twins thanked him and said good-bye. On their way they passed the classroom where Nan was making her plaited rug. They decided to peek inside. To the twins' amazement their sister was still there. Nan was alone, working on the large, oval rug which she was going to give to Dinah for her birthday.

Flossie and Freddie decided not to disturb her, because they were afraid she might ask them why they had come down to Lake Metoka. But she heard them and turned around.

"Hello," she said.

"We thought we'd come down and see what's going on," Freddie spoke up quickly. "Let's see your rug."

Nan was very glad to show her lovely work, but she made the twins promise that they would not tell anyone at home about it. She said it was to be a surprise for somebody in the house.

"We all have secrets, don't we?" Flossie giggled. Then, at a look from Freddie, she blushed and added, "We won't tell anybody about your secret, Nan."

The older girl showed them how she was sewing the plaits together in her half-finished rug.

"Why, there's a picture in it!" Flossie exclaimed.

Nan nodded. "Can you tell what it is?" she asked.

The small twins studied the pattern for a few seconds, then Freddie said, "It's going to be a cat in front of a fireplace."

This was exactly right. Nan still had to put the tail on the cat and finish the border in gay colours.

"The border's awfully pretty," Flossie said. "The colours all go the same way, don't they?"

Nan said that was the way she had planned it.

"How do you make plaits?" Flossie asked her.

Nan said if Flossie would follow her to the side of the room where the board was, she would show her where the girls had pinned the strips of wool to plait them.

But Flossie was not satisfied with this. She wanted to plait something herself, so Nan found three strips of wool, pinned them down tightly, and let her little sister's chubby fingers start to plait them.

Freddie was not the least bit interested in trying to plait anything. He wandered around and finally came back to Nan's rug, which lay on a table. Looking at it, he thought Nan must have finished the part she was doing.

"It's time to put in some different colours," Freddie judged.

Finding another plait on the table, he decided to fasten it on.

"But first I'll have to cut off the plait that's hanging on there," he said, and found a pair of scissors.

Holding up the plait which Nan had been sewing to the rug, he snipped it off cleanly and threw it in the wastebasket. Then he picked up the other plait. Finding a pin, he put the two pieces together.

"That doesn't look right either," the little boy told himself.

Wondering what he ought to do now, he looked around. On the next table lay a plait for another girl's rug with completely different colours. The little boy decided this might be pretty in Nan's rug, so he helped himself to it.

He pinned this plait on to the other, but thought it did not look well. Instead of taking the pins out, he decided to cut the plait off.

Snip went the scissors!

"It still looks funny," the little boy thought.

Snip went the scissors again!

A moment later Nan and Flossie walked back. Seeing what had happened, their eyes grew very large.

"Freddie, what in the world have you done?" Nan cried.

Freddie told her, adding that he hoped he had not done anything wrong.

"You've cut off the cat's tail!" Flossie exclaimed.

Unfortunately, he had. Nan measured the two pieces which he had snipped.

"They're too short to use!" she screamed. "And what am I going to tell the girl at the next table?"

Freddie was too stunned to speak.

"What did you do with the first piece you cut off my rug?" Nan asked him sternly.

Freddie pointed to the wastebasket. Nan reached in and picked up the plait.

Alas! Someone had spilled ink in the wastebasket. Now it was all over the plait.

Tears came to Nan's eyes. "Freddie, you've ruined my rug!" she sobbed.

CHAPTER VII

A STOLEN PRIZE

AS Freddie stared at the plait covered with ink, he felt very sorry. Looking up at Nan, in a very small voice he said:

"Nan, please, take some of my clothes to make new rags for your rug."

"Your clothes? Why, Mother wouldn't let me cut up your clothes," Nan said, drying her eyes.

Freddie could think of nothing he might do to make up for the damage he had caused. But by the next morning Flossie had an idea for him. She asked Freddie to go up to the attic with her.

"All our winter clothes are put away," she said. "And I know where there's an old coat of mine we can use for Nan's rug."

The twins climbed the stairs to the attic, and Flossie opened the door to the big cupboard. Inside were rows and rows of clothes in bags. She felt among them until she came to one which was short.

"I'm sure this is my coat," she said, and ripped

51

the paper off. Indeed it was—a navy blue one which Flossie had nearly outgrown.

The little girl took the coat off the hanger and carried it to her room.

"I'll ask Mother if I may cut it up for Nan's rug," she said. But Mrs. Bobbsey was not at home.

Dinah was in the basement washing clothes, so Flossie decided not to bother her.

"I'm sure it will be all right," she told Freddie. "Do you want to find some scissors and help me rip the seams?"

Freddie thought this would be fun, and besides, it would make up to Nan for what he had done the day before. He found two pairs of small scissors, and the children got to work.

First the sleeves came out. Then the collar came off. As Freddie started to rip the under-arm seams, Flossie put her scissors into the hem at the bottom of the coat. She had ripped about three inches of this, when suddenly her fingers felt something hard at the bottom of the coat. Putting her hand down inside, she pulled out a penny!

"Look, Freddie! Look!" she cried excitedly. "We can put this with our goldfish money."

"Maybe there's some more," Freddie suggested, and reached in.

He came up with a nickel. Flossie quickly ripped more of the hem, and ran her hand along the inside. She found ten cents more. But that was all. Freddie offered to run to the garage with the coins and put them in their secret box.

While he was gone, Flossie finished ripping the seams. Freddie had just returned to the room when they heard footsteps on the stairs. A moment later Mrs. Bobbsey appeared in the doorway. Seeing the pieces of blue cloth lying on Flossie's bed, she asked why the children had ripped the coat apart. They told her.

"You've cut up your coat?" Mrs. Bobbsey gasped. "It was perfectly good for a play coat for next winter, Flossie."

"But we wanted to help Nan," the little girl explained pleadingly.

"What I should do is make you sew it together again, but I'm afraid it wouldn't look just right," Mrs. Bobbsey said with a sigh. "Hereafter *don't* take your clothes apart until you get my permission."

The twins said they were sorry. But what about Nan and the material she needed?

Mrs. Bobbsey went to the attic herself and found a dress which was too small for Flossie. It happened to be a navy blue also and when she told the twins they might take it to Nan, they were very happy, and trotted off.

When Freddie and Flossie arrived at the rug-making class, Mrs. Shole invited them to come in and sit down, but the twins did not want to do this. They merely wanted to leave the old dress with Nan, they said.

Their sister was delighted to have it, and said now she could fix up the rug so the pattern would be the same all round the edge.

"And the cat can have a tail after all," Flossie remarked.

When they heard this the other girls laughed and crowded around to see the picture on Nan's rug. All this time Freddie was tugging at Flossie's hand. Finally he whispered:

"Come on! I saw the boys getting ready to put their boats in the water."

He and Flossie ran from the rug-making class to the shore of the lake. The stake with the cable and bridle attached was already in the water. One of the boys was just fastening his boat to it. A moment later he started the motor, and away went his little craft. Round and round it circled.

"It's not going very fast," Freddie remarked to his twin. "I hope when Bert gets his motor it will go much faster."

Flossie went over to Bert and repeated this. But it did not seem to make him happy. He said he probably could not get a motor. Even with the extra money he had earned, Bert was afraid he could not possibly get enough in time to be in the race.

"Freddie and I have some money that we——" Flossie began. Then she stopped. She had almost given the secret away!

The little girl felt she must tell someone about the money she and Freddie had found in the coat that morning. Seeing Mr. Warren go into the classroom, Flossie skipped after him. On the way, she noticed a boy scoot around the corner of the building and dash off as if he were trying to get away from someone.

"Why, that's Danny Rugg!" she told herself. "I thought he'd gone to camp at Whitesail Harbour. He probably made up the whole story."

Although Danny had his back to Flossie, she was sure he was holding something large in his arms, and wondered what it was. Since Danny was always doing mean things, he probably had been up to some tricks during the past few minutes.

A moment later Flossie forgot about Danny. As she entered the classroom, Mr. Warren cried out:

"My boat is gone!"

Flossie stared. "What boat?" she asked.

"The *Challenger,* my prize boat!"

The teacher said it was gone from the glass case. He had left the case unlocked after showing the boat to the boys that morning. Now it was gone!

"I'm awfully sorry," Flossie said, adding, "Maybe one of the boys borrowed it."

Mr. Warren dashed from the room towards the lake, with Flossie at his heels. Not seeing the *Challenger* on the lake, he asked each of his pupils if he knew anything about the missing boat.

"No, sir," each one answered.

"Is it gone?" Bert asked.

Looking very worried, the teacher exclaimed, "My prize boat has been stolen!"

CHAPTER VIII

BERT'S CLUE

IT was not until the middle of the afternoon that Flossie suddenly remembered having seen Danny Rugg running away from the recreation building. She was sure he had been carrying something large in his arms.

Could it have been the *Challenger?*

She ran to find Bert, who was in the room over the garage, putting finishing touches on his speed-boat. He had worked in his father's lumber-yard after class had ended in the morning, but when there was no more work for him to do, Mr. Bobbsey had suggested that he go home.

"Bert!" Flossie cried, when she was halfway up the stairs, "maybe Danny Rugg took Mr. Warren's boat!"

As the little girl reached the top step, Bert turned around and looked at her in surprise.

"He couldn't have taken it," Bert replied. "Danny has gone to Whitesail Harbour."

"I don't think so," Flossie insisted. "I'm sure I saw him out by the lake."

"Today?"

"Yes," Flossie answered.

Bert was amazed. He said he would go over to Danny's house at once and check up. He set his own boat on the workbench, and hurried down the stairs. It was not a long way to Danny's house, and Bert ran most of the distance.

Reaching the house, he rang the doorbell. It was several minutes before the door was opened by Danny's mother.

"How do you do, Mrs. Rugg?" Bert said politely. "Has Danny gone to camp yet?"

"No, he hasn't," she answered. "Mr. Rugg and I are going to drive him there, but we haven't been able to go yet, because Mr. Rugg has had important business to attend to. Is there something you would like me to tell Danny? He went on an errand for me this morning and hasn't returned. Probably met some boys and had lunch with them."

Bert was a little taken aback. He had been so sure that Flossie was wrong about seeing Danny, that now he could not find an excuse for having come to the house. Finally he said that he would like to talk to Danny about boats because he was going to Whitesail Harbour.

"Does Danny have a boat?" Bert asked.

Mrs. Rugg shook her head. "I don't believe so," she said. "But I can't be sure. Danny has had a good many toys in his life, and he may have a boat that I don't remember."

Bert could think of nothing more to say, so he decided to leave. He told Mrs. Rugg that he would come to see Danny later.

As he reached the sidewalk, Bert decided not to go home but to walk downtown to see if he could find Danny. Meeting a couple of boys he knew, he asked if they had seen him.

"Not for a couple of hours," one of the boys answered, "but I did notice him down here this morning."

"Where?" Bert wanted to know.

The boy thought for a moment and then said he seemed to remember Danny was going into a toy store. As Bert started to move away, the boy laughingly added:

"Are you and Danny having trouble again?"

Bert Bobbsey grinned. "Not—yet," he answered. Then he ran down the street and went into the toy store. Since he knew the owner of the store well, he did not mind asking if Danny had been there and bought anything that day.

"He was here but he didn't buy anything," the man answered.

"What was he looking at?" Bert asked.

"Danny was very interested in midget speed-boats. I don't happen to have any. But he told me there's going to be a great race at Whitesail Harbour, where he's going to camp, and he was hoping to enter the race."

Bert thanked the toy-store man for the information and hurried outside. When he reached the sidewalk, he stood still, wondering if Danny really had taken Mr. Warren's prize boat. And if he had, where would he most likely be trying it out?

After several minutes' thought, Bert concluded that the ideal place would be Dooran's Pond in a woods just outside Lakeport. Immediately he decided to go there and see if Danny were around.

"I think I'll ask Charlie to go along," Bert decided, and went into a store to use the telephone.

Fortunately Charlie was at home and agreed at once to meet Bert with his bicycle and accompany him. Bert hurried home to get his own bicycle, and the two boys rode off.

Reaching the edge of the woods, they left their bicycles at the home of a boy they knew and trudged along a path through the trees. The pond, a private one, was a pretty good size. It was never used for swimming, because it was stocked with goldfish.

As Bert and Charlie neared the pond, they could hear splashing.

"Somebody's there," Bert whispered excitedly, and started to run on tiptoe.

Though the two boys tried to be quiet, Charlie stepped on a dead branch, which broke with a loud crack. Apparently the sound carried to the person on the edge of the pond. Before the boys could reach it, they saw a boy dash off among the trees.

"Do you think that's Danny?" Charlie asked Bert.

"I can't see him very well, but that plaid shirt he has on looks exactly like one Danny sometimes wears for school," Bert answered.

The two boys started to run, and seemed to be catching up to the fleeing figure, when suddenly the boy ahead of them disappeared. Where could he have gone? Bert and Charlie looked in the bushes and then up among the tree branches, but could not see Danny or anyone else. Hurrying a little farther along the trail, they came to a cave. The grass in front of it seemed to be trampled.

"I'll bet Danny's in there," Bert whispered. "Let's look."

At first Charlie hesitated, because he thought a wild animal might be living in the cave. But when Bert said he would run in alone, Charlie consented to go along.

The two boys got down on their hands and knees and crawled inside. At first they could see nothing because the light was so dim. But when their eyes became accustomed to the darkness, they learned that Danny was not inside. Nor was there anyone else.

"Well, I guess he's gone," Bert sighed. "Let's go to Danny's house. Maybe he's home by this time. And if he has the boat, we can find out about it."

The boys returned to the house where they had left their bicycles and rode back to Lakeport.

Reaching Danny's home, they stood their bicycles against the kerb, and went up the front-porch steps.

When Bert rang the bell this time, Danny himself answered it. He did not greet the boys as if he were glad to see them. Instead he said:

"What do you mean checking up on me 'cause I didn't go to camp when I said?"

"I wasn't checking up on you," Bert answered. "I just came to ask you about speedboats up at Whitesail Harbour. Are you going to take a boat along and go in the race?"

"What's it to you if I do?" Danny sneered.

Bert flushed angrily, but Charlie started to laugh. "You're not a bit polite, Danny," he said. "Why don't you invite us into your house when we come to call on you?"

With this Charlie shoved the door open a little more. In that second he saw a midget boat standing on the hall table. Could it be the *Challenger*? A moment later Danny Rugg slammed the door in the boys' faces.

CHAPTER IX

GIRL DETECTIVES

AS Bert and Charlie hurried away from Danny's house, Charlie said excitedly, "Bert, I think I saw the *Challenger* on the hall table there!"

"You did?" Bert cried. "Then I'm going right back."

He turned around and leaped up the steps. But though he rang the doorbell a long time, no one came to answer it. Finally he gave up.

"Did it really look like Mr. Warren's boat?" Bert asked Charlie, as the two boys walked towards the Bobbsey house.

Charlie shrugged. He said it was not very light in the Rugg hall, but from a quick glance the boat certainly did look like the *Challenger*. Bert could not get the episode out of his mind, and told the rest of his family about it later that day.

Dinah was very much disturbed. After thinking the whole thing over, she suddenly chuckled to herself. Calling Freddie and Flossie to her directly after breakfast the next morning, she said to them:

"Why don't you two children go to Danny's house and try to sell some goldfish? You will probably be able to get inside and you can look around and see if Danny has that stolen boat."

Flossie clapped her hands. Freddie stuck out his chest and declared he was going to be a detective. From the time Freddie had been very small, he had always imitated men with exciting jobs.

First, he had wanted to be a fireman. Then he had wanted to be the captain of a boat. One time he had wanted to be a policeman, and now he was to be a detective.

"If Danny's got that boat, I'll find it!" he declared. "Come on, Flossie! Let's get our fish."

They had four left from the day before. Eagerly they carried them to the Rugg home and rang the doorbell. Danny himself came to the door. Seeing the small Bobbsey twins, he looked surprised. Then he spied the box.

"So you think you're going to sell me some goldfish, eh?" he said unpleasantly.

"How do you know we're selling goldfish?" Flossie asked him.

"Well, I found out," the older boy said. "You kids are silly to buy goldfish to sell. I know a place where you can get all you want for nothing."

"Where is it?"

But Danny would not tell them. He said his family did not want goldfish anyway, so the children should run along. But Freddie had no intention of leaving so soon. He had really come there to be a detective, and he had work to do.

For a moment the little boy wondered how he could get into the house. Danny had the door open about a foot, and was blocking the entrance. Suddenly Freddie leaned down and ducked between Danny's legs, upsetting the bigger boy.

"Hey, what are you doing?" Danny cried as he scrambled to his feet. Seeing Freddie run from the hall to the living-room, he exclaimed, "Where you going? Get out of here!"

All this time Freddie's eyes were darting from place to place. There was no boat in sight. He decided it must be upstairs in Danny's bedroom.

As the older boy chased him through the dining-room and kitchen, Freddie came back to the hall. An instant later he was dashing up the stairs.

Mrs. Rugg, who was on the second floor, heard the commotion. She hurried to the stairs, just as Freddie reached the top step. She grabbed his shoulder.

"What are you up to, Freddie?" Mrs. Rugg asked severely. "Did Danny invite you to come up?"

Freddie had to admit that he had run up by himself.

"Then I think you'd better leave at once," Mrs. Rugg told him.

Freddie turned and went downstairs. Flossie was standing in the hall wide-eyed. Danny laughed uproariously, shoved the children out, and slammed the door after them.

"He's a horrid boy," Flossie remarked, as the twins started for home. "Freddie, did you see the boat while you were inside the house?"

"No. What do you think we ought to do?"

Flossie had no solution to their problem. Sighing, she said she guessed they would have to leave it to the grown-ups.

When they reached home, the two children went at once to talk to Dinah. After telling her what had happened when they tried to sell goldfish, Freddie asked:

"Where do you suppose that place is Danny said you could get goldfish for nothing?"

Dinah did not know, so a little later when Sam came into the kitchen, Freddie asked him. At once the kindly Negro said he was sure it was Dooran's Pond.

"Why, that's where Bert went to see if Danny was sailing the *Challenger*!" Freddie exclaimed.

That noon Mr. Bobbsey told his family there was going to be a special unloading of lumber from a ship on Lake Metoka. Freddie said he wanted to see it, and Bert would, of course, be there anyway.

Flossie said she did not want to go because she had something very important on her mind. She wished Nan would not go either. She wanted Nan to go some place with her.

"Where is it?" Freddie asked his twin.

"To Dooran's Pond," Flossie replied. Then she

whispered to Freddie, "I want to see if I can find some free goldfish to sell."

Now Freddie was torn between a desire to go to the lumber-yard and watch, because he always loved to see boats being unloaded, or to go to the pond with Flossie. It was even possible that Danny might be sailing the *Challenger* there.

"I wish I could go to Dooran's Pond," Bert said, "but I have to be at the lumber-yard and earn some money. Time is getting short for me to buy the motor." He looked rather sad and added with a sigh, "I'm afraid I'm not going to be able to do it, though."

"It will be a shame if you can't," Nan told him. "I wish I had some money to give you, but you know I spent all I saved."

The others knew what she meant. Nan was a very kind-hearted girl and had emptied her own piggy bank to give money to a girl who needed it to buy a ticket for a school play.

"Flossie," she said, "suppose you and I go to Dooran's Pond alone. If we see Danny there with the *Challenger,* we'll come back and tell the boys."

So their brothers went one direction while the girls took another. Nan and Flossie rode on a bus to the woods where the pond was. Then they walked towards the water. When they were about twenty-five feet from the pond, in a spot which was heavily wooded, two boys suddenly jumped out from among the bushes and blocked their path.

"You can't go any farther," one of them said gruffly.

"And why not?" Nan asked coolly, standing her ground.

"We don't have to tell you why," the boy said. "You go on back where you came from."

Flossie was frightened. The boys were big, and looked as if they might hit the girls if they did not obey.

Nan thought for a moment. She had to protect Flossie, and did not want to have any trouble with the boys. On the other hand, having recognized them as friends of Danny's from the next town, she was certain Danny was at the pond. The two boys were acting as guards to keep people away. It looked as if Danny must be doing something he shouldn't. Could he be sailing the stolen boat?

Suddenly Nan had an idea. Taking Flossie's hand, she said, "All right, we'll leave."

"And don't come back!" one of the boys warned as the Bobbsey girls moved away from the spot.

Flossie was sorry that they were going. She had hoped to find out if there were any goldfish in the pond, and maybe sometime soon she could get Dinah to bring her and Freddie out to get a few of them.

About a hundred feet beyond, Nan suddenly stopped. She smiled at her younger sister and said:

"Flossie, we're going back now!"

"You really mean it?" the little girl asked in surprise. "I'm afraid the boys will hurt us."

Nan told her that they were not going back by the path. They would zigzag through the woods and come to the pond on the other side.

"We'll fool the boys," she said.

"Goody. Serves 'em right," Flossie answered.

The sisters had almost reached the pond when suddenly a squirrel jumped out of a tree directly in front of Flossie. The little girl was frightened and screamed before she thought.

Like a shot the two boy guards came running around the pond in their direction. Nan and Flossie knew they would have to flee, but as Nan turned to go, she caught a glimpse of another boy at the edge of the pond. He was leaning down, just ready to push a small boat into the water. Nan was sure the boy was Danny but she did not dare to wait to find out.

"Run fast!" she urged Flossie.

CHAPTER X

A PLAYGROUND FIGHT

IN their race to get away from the boys, Flossie stumbled over a tree root and skinned a knee, while Nan caught her hair in a brier bush and cried:

"Ouch!"

But in spite of their hurts, they managed to get to a main road ahead of the two boys who were chasing them. Just then a bus came along and the two girls climbed aboard. They sat down panting.

"Oh, I was awful scared. Weren't you, Nan?" Flossie asked.

Nan admitted she was glad they had slipped away from the boys. She was sorry, however, that they had failed to find out anything about Mr. Warren's missing boat. She was sure she had seen Danny with a boat at the edge of the pond.

"But maybe we can find out some other way," Flossie suggested.

When they reached home, she went to the basement to talk to Dinah. After telling the cook what had happened, the little girl said:

"It was a big disappointment, Dinah. I wanted to get some free goldfish out of the pond so that Freddie and I could sell them and make more money."

The kindly woman shook her head. "It's a good thing you didn't take any of the fish in that pond," she said. "They're not free. They belong to Mr. Dooran and I'm sure he wouldn't want anybody to take them away."

Flossie sighed. "Then Freddie and I'll just have to buy our fish at the pet shop after all."

Next morning the small twins went downtown to get more goldfish. This was their last chance to make money for Bert. Tonight Daddy Bobbsey would decide whether or not the boy might have a motor in his midget speedboat.

"We have to make lots of sales today," Flossie told the pet-shop owner. "So I think we'd better buy extra fish."

"Where are you going to sell them?" Mr. Rodin asked.

Flossie explained that Sam was going to drive her and Freddie to the playground on the other side of town. None of the children who went there to play lived in the neighbourhood where Freddie and Flossie had sold the fish before. The twins were sure many of the children would be interested in buying fish.

"I hope they'll spend their lollipop money for goldfish," Flossie said seriously.

The man smiled. He said certainly the enjoyment one got out of goldfish lasted much longer than that from a lollipop. He gave them a special rate after they told him this was to be the last day they would buy his fish, and wished them good luck as they left the store.

In a few minutes Sam stopped for the twins and drove them to the playground. He made them promise not to leave the grounds until he came back to pick them up.

"And be careful when you play. Don't get any more skinned knees, Flossie," he added with a grin. Flossie was still wearing patches on her knees.

The twins walked up to a group of children at a sandbox. But they were not playing in the sand. They were gathered near a tall boy who was showing them something. As the Bobbseys came closer, Freddie gasped.

"Why, that's Danny Rugg!" he whispered.

He and Flossie walked closer. To their dismay they heard Danny say:

"I've got the most beautiful goldfish in the world to sell—and they're cheap, too. Only ten cents each. Who wants to buy some?"

For a few minutes Freddie and Flossie were too stunned to speak. Then both of them became angry. They were sure that Danny had taken the fish from Dooran's Pond and Dinah had said this was not right.

"It's not fair," Freddie declared. "How can we sell fish if Danny sells his cheaper?"

Freddie walked directly up to Danny and tapped him on the arm. The older boy's eyes flashed angrily as he saw the boxes of fish in Freddie's and Flossie's arms.

"I got here first," he said. "You can't sell your fish."

"We can, too!" Freddie told him. "And anyway we bought our fish and you didn't. You stole them from Mr. Dooran!"

As Freddie said this, the other children gasped. They stared at the small twins and at Danny. Finally one boy spoke up, saying he would not buy anything that was stolen. His dad had told him this was against the law.

"I didn't steal these fish!" Danny shouted.

Setting down his box, he grabbed hold of Freddie's shoulders and shook him so hard the little boy could barely see. Flossie was fearful. She grasped Danny's coat and pulled it hard—so hard, in fact, that the pocket ripped a little.

"Leave my brother alone!" the small girl cried, tears coming to her eyes. She was so afraid Freddie was going to be hurt.

"Why don't you pick on somebody your size?" asked a boy named Dave, who was looking on.

When Danny sneered, Dave walked up and gave him a shove. With that two other boys ran forward. But they were friends of Danny's, and at once started a fight. Fists flew. All of them fell to the ground, rolled over, and got up again.

"Freddie!" Flossie screamed, and dragged him away.

But Freddie was the one Danny was after. Seeing an opening, he made a dive for the little fellow and grabbed him by the legs. Down Freddie went, hitting the ground hard. Danny was just about to give him a punch, when a girl cried:

"Here comes Mr. West, the teacher!"

Hurrying across the grass was the director of the playground. He was a young, athletic man, who looked as if he would not tolerate any nonsense. Quickly the fighters scattered in various directions. Danny left in such a hurry that he forgot his fish.

When Mr. West reached the group, he asked what had happened. Flossie told him, since Freddie was sobbing—his ear hurt from hitting the ground.

"You shouldn't have accused Danny of stealing the fish," the director said, "unless you knew it for sure. On the other hand, Danny should not have started a fight."

When everything was calm again, Freddie and Flossie asked Mr. West if it would be all right for them to sell their goldfish. He said, "Go ahead."

In a few minutes the small twins had sold every fish they had brought, and were sorry that they did not have more.

When the fish were gone, Flossie asked Mr. West what was going to happen to the goldfish

Danny had brought. He said he did not know. Could the children tell him where Danny lived?

"Yes," Freddie answered. "But the fish don't belong to Danny. We're sure he stole them from Dooran's Pond."

"Would you like Freddie and me to take the fish back there and put them in the water?" Flossie offered.

Mr. West said that under the circumstances he believed he had better take charge of the fish himself. He would find out from Mr. Dooran whether the fish had come from his pond.

"They're large, unusual varieties," he said. "Mr. Dooran should be able to identify them."

"We wish you could find out something else," Freddie spoke up. He had stopped crying now. "Mr. Warren's boat—it's called the *Challenger*—is gone. We've been hunting for it. We think maybe Danny—borrowed it."

The playground director looked thoughtful for several seconds. "If you're right," he said, "Danny is a problem. I'll find out what I can."

"Thank you," the twins said, and went off to play.

When Sam came for them, he looked at Freddie's torn clothes and asked what in the world he had been up to. Hearing that Danny was at the bottom of this recent fracas, he frowned.

"I'll sure be glad when that Danny goes to camp," he said.

Sam was pleased to learn that the small twins

had sold all their fish, and asked them how much money they had.

"We haven't counted it yet," Flossie answered. "Will you help us when we get home?"

Sam said he would be glad to. As soon as they reached home, the twins got their secret box from the garage and carried it to the kitchen. They spread the money on the table, and Sam counted it.

"Two dollars," he announced. "That's mighty fine that you children got all this money for Bert."

"I think so, too," Dinah said, smiling. She was preparing a lunch of bacon, macaroni and cheese, and also fruit pudding.

During the afternoon Freddie and Flossie could hardly keep their secret. They still had the box of money hidden in the garage, and before supper-time they made at least ten trips to be sure it was still there.

Bert came home with his father, and immediately went to his room to bring down his midget speed-boat. The other members of the family had not seen it for several days, because Bert had taken it back to class to put the finishing touches to it. Now Bert proudly carried it into the living-room where the others were gathered. Everyone gasped.

"Bert, your boat's stunning!" Nan cried.

"Boy, I bet that could win a race if it had a motor!" Freddie exclaimed.

Mr. and Mrs. Bobbsey said Bert had certainly

done a very fine job on the boat. It looked as perfect as many they had seen in stores.

All this time Bert had not said a word. He was waiting for his father to tell him whether or not the boat was worthy of a motor. Finally Mr. Bobbsey spoke.

"Bert, I'm very proud of the job you've done, and I'm also pleased that you have worked so hard at the lumber-yard. How much did you earn down there?"

"Three dollars," Bert answered.

"Well, as I told you, I will give you five dollars," his father told him. "That makes eight all together. You ought to be able to get a small motor for that price."

Bert stood very still. He had not moved a muscle of his face. As a matter of fact, he was trying not to cry. He knew that the cheapest motor which would be good would cost twelve dollars. He had failed to attain his goal!

"I—I'm afraid I can't get it, Dad," he said. "I'll need four dollars more."

Before Mr. Bobbsey could reply, Freddie and Flossie decided it was time for them to speak up. The two of them rushed up to their brother and grabbed hold of him.

"Bert, we have a wonderful surprise for you!" Flossie cried.

"It's money," Freddie said gleefully, "from the goldfish!"

He pulled a handful of coins from one pocket.

Flossie could not wait. She put a hand into another of Freddie's pockets, and brought out the rest. They handed the two dollars to Bert.

Their brother looked at them amazed. He did not understand, he said. Excitedly the small twins explained their secret. When they finished, Bert hugged the two of them so hard that they both squealed. He was too overcome to speak.

Tears stood in Mrs. Bobbsey's eyes also. "You darling children," she said.

Freddie and Flossie came in for a great deal of hugging and praise. Dinah and Sam, who had been standing in the hall listening, now walked in and added their commendation to that of the others.

"Oh, I almost forgot, Bert," Flossie said suddenly. "Mr. Warren's going to get you a twelve-dollar motor for ten dollars."

This was too much for Bert. "Hurrah!" he shouted, and actually jumped up and down. He could go into the race after all!

In the midst of the excitement the telephone suddenly rang. Dinah went to answer it, and a moment later stepped back into the living-room.

"Freddie, it's for you," she said. "The man from the playground wants to speak to you!"

CHAPTER XI

NAN IN THE NEWS

"HELLO, Mr. West," Freddie called excitedly into the telephone.

"Hello, Freddie. I'm afraid my news isn't very good," said the playground director. "When I went to Danny Rugg's house this afternoon, I found that he and his family had gone to Whitesail Harbour."

"Did Danny take a boat with him?" Freddie asked quickly.

Mr. West said he did not know. A neighbour of the Ruggs had told him they had left. He was sorry not to have helped Freddie, and said he certainly hoped Mr. Warren would get his boat back soon. Then the director said good-bye.

Freddie returned to the living-room and told his family what he had just heard.

"I wonder if Danny has the *Challenger*," Bert said, and added that Mr. Warren had learned nothing about his stolen boat and the police had no clues either.

"It certainly is a shame," said Mrs. Bobbsey. "By the way, Bert, aren't you going to give your boat a name?"

Her son grinned. "Now that I'm going to have a motor and can go into the race, I ought to give my boat a name," he said. "Let's think of one."

All sorts of names were suggested, but none of them seemed to fit exactly. In the end it was Dinah who came up with a name that they thought would be just right. She said the Bobbsey family was always going here and there, and probably the little boat would travel a lot too.

"So why don't you call it the *Rover*?" she suggested.

"That's a wonderful name," Nan spoke up. "Let's have a christening ceremony, just like they do for big boats." Nan had once seen a new ocean liner launched.

"Oh, yes, please let's," Flossie cried. "Can't we go down to the lake and baptize it right now?"

Mr. Bobbsey laughingly said he thought they should wait until the motor was installed. The others agreed, and it was decided that, just as soon as the motor was put in, the whole family would go down for the christening.

"Who's going to christen the *Rover*?" Freddie asked.

None of his family answered. Then Dinah said, "If I may say somethin', I believe it ought to be Bert's twin. Nobody closer than a twin."

So it was arranged that Nan would christen the

boat. This took place two afternoons later. Mr. Bobbsey left his office early, and met his family on the shore of Lake Metoka.

This was to be more than a christening. It would be the first time the new motor would be tried out. Bert was extremely excited. While waiting for the motor, he had painted the name *Rover* on the side of his boat. Now as it stood on the shore waiting to be launched, he decided it really was a very fine-looking boat.

Dinah and Sam had come along, and now Dinah walked up and handed Nan a little bottle of white grape juice.

"When they launch a boat, they always break a bottle on it as it goes into the water," she said. "So Bert's boat must have a very proper launching."

"That's right, Dinah," said Mr. Bobbsey, "only, Nan, you'd better not break the bottle. Just sprinkle a few drops of juice on the boat."

Nan took the bottle and stood waiting. Bert said, "Ready!" and his twin poured the juice on the boat as it slid into the water.

"I christen thee *Rover*," she said.

Everyone clapped. Then Bert stepped into the water and started the motor.

Putt-putt it went. Bert released the lever which would make the boat move forward. Away it went at a good speed along the shore.

"Oh, it works!" Flossie cried excitedly.

Bert had not permitted his boat to go very fast, because he did not want it to get away. He dashed down the beach, waded out, and met the *Rover*. He picked up the boat, turned off the motor, and waded back.

"We must go home now," Mrs. Bobbsey said when Bert returned to the group. "Bert, dear, I wish you lots of luck in the race."

The race was to be held the last day of the craft classes. In the meantime, the other hobby groups were getting ready to exhibit the things they had made.

Nan had finished the rug which she planned to give Dinah for her birthday. Nobody could see where Freddie had cut off some of the plaits and nearly ruined the rug. The cat sitting by the fireplace looked very lifelike.

"Dad," said Nan at supper that evening, "I just loved my rug-making class. I'd like to go into the next session and learn to make something else."

Her father smiled, then said, "Well, dear, I'm afraid you'll have to postpone it. I'm thinking of taking my family on a little trip. Maybe you can join one of the classes later in the summer."

The twins wanted to know about the trip, but Mr. Bobbsey said he was not sure yet where it would be. Several shipments of lumber were coming in at various points, and he wanted to inspect them with a view to buying some of it. He had not yet decided to which place he would go first.

"After I decide, I'll tell you," he said.

The twins always looked forward to going on a

trip, but at the moment, Nan's and Bert's thoughts were on the exhibition, which would last several days, and the midget speedboat race. When the first day of the exhibition came, there was a good crowd to look at the various objects the pupils had made. Among these people was a photographer from the *Lakeport News*.

Unknown to the children, the head of the craft classes had arranged for a group of judges to pick out the best article in each class. The photographer was to take a picture of it, to be printed in the paper together with a story.

Towards the end of the morning a girl came up to Nan Bobbsey and told her that Mrs. Shole wanted to see her right away. Nan, who had been looking at another exhibit, hurried off. Reaching the room, she found the teacher smiling.

"Nan," she said, "your plaited rug has been chosen as the best one. The judges say the reason they picked yours is because it has such an interesting picture on it."

How happy and excited Nan was! The next thing she knew, the photographer was taking a picture of her standing alongside the plaited rug. He even got the story that she was giving it to Dinah for her birthday.

"Dinah's birthday is day after tomorrow," Nan said. "But I guess it won't matter if you print the story now. Thank you very much."

It was an odd way to present a birthday present —showing a picture of the gift first—but Nan had

a lot of fun doing it that way. When the newspaper
came early the next morning, she rushed to Dinah
and said:

"Happy Birthday!"

Of course Dinah looked surprised, and did not
understand until Nan made her read the story
under the picture in the paper.

"Well, bless you, child!" Dinah exclaimed, a
wide grin spreading over her face. Then she added,
"Nan, you were so sweet to make this rug for me.
And I'll specially prize it, because it's got all the
Bobbseys in it."

Freddie, who was standing near by, wanted to
know what she meant. Dinah laughed. "Why,
don't you remember, honey child, that there's a
piece of everybody's clothes in this rug?"

Dinah decided the occasion called for an extra-
special breakfast, but when it was ready, Bert could

not be found. Nan went into the back yard and called, but he did not answer. Finally the family gave up and sat down to eat without him.

"Maybe he went to try out the *Rover* 'cause this is the day of the race," Freddie suggested.

But Bert was not at the lake. All this time he had been working in the room above the garage. Bert knew from the trial run the day before that his boat never could win the race. And he so much wanted to win it and go into the Interstate Competition!

The boy had arisen very early, and carried his boat out to the shop. He felt that probably the trouble was not with the motor, but with the boat itself.

Taking a chance, Bert had decided that he would sharpen the prow and the keel, so that the boat could cut through the water more swiftly. Now he had finished this job, but he still had to varnish the hull.

Bert had heard his twin calling him from the yard, but had decided he must finish his job before eating breakfast. Hoping that he had guessed right about what was the matter with the speed of his boat, the boy put on the finishing touches of varnish. Then, looking at it fondly, he whispered:

"*Rover,* I sure hope you win the race!"

CHAPTER XII

A BOAT RACE

"I'M sorry to be late, Mother," Bert said, coming to the breakfast table.

When he explained what he had been doing, his mother excused him. This was to be a happy day, and everyone was in a gay mood.

"How many boys are going to be in the race?" Freddie asked.

Bert said that an elimination race had been held the day before, and that the *Rover* and two other boats were in the final.

"The other two fellows' speedboats are pretty fast," Bert added.

"But so's the *Rover*," Freddie declared.

By the time the contestants arrived at the lake with their parents and friends, Mr. Warren had the pole planted firmly in the water. He announced that each boy would be given three tries with his midget speedboat. The teacher had the boys draw numbers, and Bert was third.

"All set?" Mr. Warren asked.

The boy who had drawn first place nodded. He attached his boat, a very good-looking one, to the cable and bridle, and set it in motion.

Click went the stop-watch of a friend of Mr. Warren's who was going to time the race. When the boy's boat had gone in a circle three times, the man clicked the stop-watch again and wrote a figure down in a little book.

The next boy had his turn, then Bert walked into the water to attach the *Rover* to the cable and bridle. Around and around went Bert's boat as the Bobbseys cheered. Then the timer wrote some more numbers in his book, and the three contestants waited eagerly for the results.

But when they were announced, Bert's face fell. His boat had made the slowest time.

"Don't be discouraged," Mr. Warren said, "you have two more tries. Sometimes these boats are better after they warm up."

It almost seemed as if the *Rover* had heard Mr. Warren speak. On the second round it beat out the second boat by two seconds. On the third try the *Rover* seemed to gather tremendous speed. Away it whizzed.

"Oh, I just know it's the fastest!" Flossie cried, grabbing Nan's hand.

Nan held her breath, as the man with the stop-watch whispered to Mr. Warren. Everyone else became quiet, too. Then the teacher held up his hand and said:

"This was certainly a very close race, and I must congratulate all three contestants in it. It is my great pleasure to announce that the winner will be allowed to enter the County Race which will be held one week from today. That boy will be—Bert Bobbsey!"

Everybody clapped. Bert was so excited that he was not sure he had heard right. But a second later when his father also congratulated him, and his mother kissed him, and Nan gave him a hug, and the little twins tried to jump on his shoulders, he knew that he had heard the announcement correctly. He was the winner!

After a newspaper photographer took Bert's picture with his little boat, the boy said to him, "If it hadn't been for my little brother and sister, I never could have been in this race."

Of course, the man wanted to know what Bert meant, so he told the story of how Freddie and Flossie had sold the goldfish to make money which he needed to buy the engine for the *Rover*. The photographer insisted upon taking their pictures also.

"Only we ought to have some goldfish with us," Flossie said.

After most of the people had left, Mr. and Mrs. Bobbsey stepped up to Mr. Warren and thanked him for being so kind and giving Bert so much help. They said their son had really surprised them by making such a fine boat. They had not expected that he could build one which would be a winner.

"To tell you the truth, Bert and the other two boys in the race surprised me, too," Mr. Warren said. "I've been running classes for several summers. These boats are the best I have ever seen boys make. They ought to do well in bigger races."

Before leaving for home, Mrs. Bobbsey invited the teacher to have supper with them the following Monday evening. He gladly accepted.

When Monday arrived, the small twins mentioned that they hoped Mr. Warren would tell them about the races his *Challenger* had won.

"Since it has been stolen," Mrs. Bobbsey said, "maybe he won't want to talk about his boat."

The twins promised not to bring up the subject, and did not make a mistake. Mr. Warren, however, brought up the subject himself. He said he felt very bad about his boat being gone, but he was sure that it would turn up some time.

"How fast could it go?" Freddie asked.

The teacher said that the last race which he had won, the boat had gone sixty miles an hour.

"If I had my boat back, and if I had time to go to Whitesail Harbour, which I haven't," the teacher smiled, "I'd put the *Challenger* in the race there."

Bert now asked, "Didn't you say, Mr. Warren, that the winner of the County Race here would be entitled to race at Whitesail Harbour?"

"Yes, I did."

There was silence at the table a few seconds. Everyone knew what Bert was thinking. How the boy wished he might win the County Race next Saturday and be privileged to go to Whitesail Harbour to race!

"It would be fun for a fellow to see the race even if he couldn't be in it," Bert spoke up finally.

Mr. Bobbsey smiled, and said he had a surprise to tell his family.

"Nan, do you remember I told you I had to inspect lumber in various places? Well, one of the places is not far from Whitesail Harbour. I'll take my family there."

"Oh, Daddy, that's wonderful!" Flossie cried. "Now we can see all the white things they sell in the harbour."

The others laughed at Flossie's excited mix-up, and told her that this was not a sale of white articles like stores held. It meant the white sails on the boats in the harbour. Flossie laughed too.

Before Mr. Warren left the house, he told Bert he would help him tune up the motor of the *Rover* so it would be speedier.

"That's great," said Bert. "Can you come to-morrow morning and work with me in the room over the garage?"

"Yes, and later we'll take the boat down to Lake Metoka and try it out."

"Thank you very much, sir," Bert said, and walked out to Mr. Warren's car with him.

During the rest of the evening Bert tried to keep his mind on the County Race the next Saturday, but thoughts of Whitesail Harbour kept popping into his mind. They also brought Danny Rugg to his mind.

Suddenly an idea came to Bert. When he said good night to Nan, he whispered:

"Just as soon as we get to Whitesail Harbour, I'm going over to Danny Rugg's camp and find out if he has the *Challenger*!"

CHAPTER XIII

THE BROKEN CARRIAGE

WHENEVER Freddie and Flossie were going on a trip, they had a great deal of fun getting ready. They talked about what play clothes they wanted to pack in their suitcases, and what toys they would take. This time Freddie announced that he did not intend to take any toys.

"You're not?" Flossie asked in surprise.

"I'm going to take goldfish instead," Freddie answered.

Flossie said "Ooo-eee" very loudly, and added that she hardly thought their mother would permit this. Freddie ran into Mrs. Bobbsey's bedroom where she was looking over her own clothes for the trip.

"Mother," he said, "I've been a very good boy lately, haven't I?"

Mrs. Bobbsey smiled. She knew Freddie was going to make some kind of request. But she was not prepared for the one which he did make.

"I don't know how goldfish would like riding in a car," she said. "There's no way to make them sit still, as you know, and the water would slosh around pretty hard."

"Couldn't Daddy drive very, very carefully?" Freddie asked.

"Your father always drives carefully," his mother told him. "But I'm afraid if we went slow enough to keep the goldfish bowl from sliding around in the car, we'd be days and days on the road getting to Whitesail Harbour. It's a long drive."

Freddie was downcast. He did not want the fish to be injured, but he did so want to take a few of them along. When Mrs. Bobbsey saw the look of disappointment on his face, she said:

"Freddie, you did such a wonderful thing helping Bert, that I think it's only right to let you take some fish."

"Oh, thank you!" Freddie shouted.

"But first there is one thing you must do," his mother went on. "Figure out a way to carry them so the tank can't slip or tip and let the water spill out."

Freddie knew that this was a big job for him, but he was determined to do it. For a whole hour he thought and thought, walking around the back yard looking into the garage, going to the basement of the house. He even opened several picture books, hunting for an idea.

The little boy could think of no way to do what his mother had asked. Finally he gave up, and went out to the front walk on his bicycle.

Fortunately for Freddie a truck came along just then and solved his problem for him. The truck was carrying bottled water. Each bottle was held inside a wooden crate to keep it from being broken.

"That's the way I'll do it!" Freddie cried, and dashed back to the basement.

He remembered seeing a small crate in which something had been delivered. After examining it, Freddie knew the crate would be just right to hold a small bowl of goldfish. Climbing the steps, Freddie found a kitchen bowl with a lid which was the same size and shape as a small tank for goldfish. He carried it to the cellar and fitted it down inside the crate. It was perfect!

"Now I'll put some fish in the bowl and try out my 'speriment' on my express wagon," he told himself, and carried the crate up to the kitchen.

Freddie had learned that goldfish should not be put into cold water from the tap, so he filled the bowl and let the water stand until it was room temperature. Meanwhile, he went to the garage to get his express wagon. He cleaned it out, and then brought it to the kitchen door.

Next Freddie found the net which the pet-shop owner had given him, and took his crated goldfish bowl to the living-room. He scooped out two of the fish and put them into the small tank.

"You're going for a ride," he told the fish. "If you like it, you'll go all the way to Whitesail Harbour."

Freddie carried the crated tank outdoors and set it squarely in the centre of his express wagon.

"We're off," the little boy said.

He pulled the wagon very gently and kept turning around to watch the effect. The water hardly moved in the tank and the fish seemed to be very content. Freddie was happy.

"Now I'll go a little faster and see what happens," he said, and started to run.

He got all the way to the corner and nothing had happened.

"I'll just take you a little farther," he told the fish, and pulled the wagon around the corner.

Now Freddie had not counted on the fact that the side street was hilly. As he trudged along, the crate began to slide towards the back of the wagon, which was tilted now. Suddenly the crate slipped to the sidewalk.

Bang!

Freddie was frightened. He almost was afraid to turn around and see what had happened. But he did. To his relief the crate had slid off and landed right side up on the sidewalk. The lid was still on the bowl and the fish did not seem to be any the worse for their tumble.

"Well, I guess that proves my invention is okay!" Freddie told himself proudly.

He picked up the crated tank and lifted it to the wagon. Then very carefully he went down the hill and turned the corner towards home. He could hardly wait to show his mother what he had made.

On the way he met Flossie wheeling her doll carriage. In it was her favourite doll, Marie, who was dressed in her prettiest clothes.

"Who made that?" Flossie asked, seeing the crate.

"I did," her twin answered, "so I can take some fish on our trip."

"That's nice," Flossie said. "I'm going to take Marie with me."

"Where you going now?" Freddie wanted to know.

"I'm going with Nan to get Dinah's birthday present," Flossie told him. "Nan'll be here in a minute."

When Nan came up she admired Freddie's invention, and then the two girls went off towards Lake Metoka to pick up the plaited rug. It was their plan to put it on the carriage to carry home.

Reaching the craft shop, the sisters met several other girls who were folding up their rugs to take home. The exhibition, which had lasted for several days, was over.

Dinah's birthday present was heavier than Nan had realized. When she rolled up the rug and laid it across the doll carriage, she had to help Flossie wheel the carriage. Moreover, each time they pushed it up and down the kerbs, the carriage refused to hold its burden. The rug kept slipping off and was getting dirty.

"I guess I'll have to carry it," Nan sighed. She picked it up and they went along for two blocks. Then Nan stopped. "This is too heavy," she said. "I just can't carry it so far."

She laid it on the carriage once more and they started off. A moment later the rug rolled on top of Marie.

"Oh, the rug's smothering my baby!" Flossie cried out.

Nan rolled the rug to the other end of the carriage, and they walked on. The next kerbstone they came to was very steep. This time Nan had to lift the carriage up to the sidewalk.

They had not rolled it far when suddenly one of the wheels collapsed. The doll hit the side of the carriage with a *smack*. The rug opened and rolled topside down on to the sidewalk!

"Now my carriage is broken!" Flossie wailed. "And your pussycat's all dirty."

"Don't cry, dear!" Nan said. "I'll see that the carriage gets fixed. And I'll wipe off the rug."

"But what are we going to do now?" Flossie asked tearfully. "We can't carry the carriage and the doll and the rug home."

Nan realized this, too. She told Flossie that she would go into a store and telephone to their mother, asking her to come and rescue them with the car. Nan asked Flossie to wait right where she was until she came back.

Flossie realized that the carriage was in the way of people coming along the sidewalk, so she dragged first the rug, then the carriage and doll to the kerbstone. Turning her back to them, she watched for Nan to return.

It was because she had her back to the street, that she did not notice a sprinkling cart coming along. Since Flossie was standing by a telegraph pole, the driver of the cart did not see her.

The next instant he opened the sprinkler system full force, and water poured from it over the little girl, the carriage the doll, and Dinah's birthday present!

CHAPTER XIV

A CLEVER RESCUE

AFTER receiving Nan's telephone call, Mrs.
Bobbsey got her car from the garage and drove to
meet her. When she arrived at the corner where
Nan had told her to come, what a sorry sight she
saw! Flossie was sobbing, and Nan looked very
unhappy.

"My dolly is ruined and the carriage is ruined,
and everything is the matter!" her mother heard
Flossie say.

Mrs. Bobbsey stopped at the kerb and jumped
out. "What has happened?" she asked.

Then she saw the wet rug, the almost ruined
doll, and the broken carriage.

"The sprinkler cart gave Flossie a bath," Nan
explained. "I've been trying to tell Flossie that the
things aren't really ruined. After they dry out,
they'll be all right."

Her mother examined all the articles, and said
Nan was right. Probably Flossie's doll needed a

shampoo anyway, and a new wheel could be put on to the doll carriage with very little expense.

"Hop in and we'll go home," Mrs. Bobbsey directed.

When they reached home, Nan carried the rug to her bedroom without letting Dinah see it. She laid it flat on the floor so that it would dry without a hump. By late afternoon it was as good as new, and Nan proudly carried it down to the kitchen to give to the faithful cook.

"Why, honey child, it's even prettier than the picture in the paper!" Dinah exclaimed. "I don't see how you made this all by yourself. It's just beautiful!" She grinned. "Why, it's 'most too pretty for me to use in our own room."

Nan insisted that she had made it for Dinah and Sam's bedroom, and that they were to enjoy the rug whenever they were there.

"I'll sure treasure this," Dinah said. "And I'll be certain to see that nothin' ever happens to it."

Later Sam told Nan that he, too, was going to enjoy looking at the rug, and he thought she had done a splendid job.

"While you all are at Whitesail Harbour," he said, "Dinah and I'll have a chance to enjoy it a special lot."

After supper that evening Mrs. Bobbsey said that she thought they would have to take a trunk to the seaside.

"We'll need several changes of clothes," she

said, "and there isn't room in the car for all of us and a lot of baggage too."

"Besides, I have to carry my goldfish," Freddie spoke up.

"And I have to take my boat," Bert reminded the others.

"And don't forget Marie," Flossie said.

Mr. Bobbsey laughed, and looked at Nan. "Aren't you taking anything?"

Nan giggled. "I'm not going to take anything, but I want to bring some things home from the sea-shore. I hope there'll be room."

It was a jolly supper hour, and later when Bert went upstairs, he began to think about the County Race on Saturday. Freddie had already gone to bed, and Bert noticed that the little boy had moved the *Rover* from the bureau to the foot of his bed.

"I certainly don't want anything to happen to the boat before Saturday," Bert told himself, as he took off his shoes. "Maybe I'd better hide it."

He could not think of any good place at the moment, but next morning he had figured out a dandy one. After breakfast he went back upstairs and picked up the *Rover*. Going into his mother's bedroom, he lifted the lid of the half-packed trunk, picked up some of the clothes, and hid the boat beneath them. Then he closed the trunk.

"I'll just tell Mother and no one else where I've hidden the boat," he thought.

Going downstairs, he learned that Mrs. Bobbsey had gone to the market. While he was waiting for her, Bert received a telephone call from Charlie Mason asking him to go to the lake with him and work on Charlie's boat. Although Charlie had not been able to make a boat good enough to go in the race, he had a nice-looking one.

"Maybe you can help me improve it, Bert," he said.

Bert willingly agreed to go, and the boys went off for about two hours. When Bert returned home, he went to his mother and told her about his own boat. A strange look came over her face.

"Did you mind, Mother?" Bert asked.

"No, Bert, it's not that, but it's too bad you didn't tell me what you'd done," she answered. "Your little boat is already on its way to Whitesail Harbour."

"What do you mean?" Bert asked.

His mother said that she had finished packing the trunk, and the expressmen had come and taken it away!

"Oh, no!" Bert cried out. "The boat's been taken away! What am I going to do?"

For answer Mrs. Bobbsey dashed to the telephone and called the express office. She only hoped that the Bobbsey trunk had not yet been put on a train. Bert waited breathlessly, saying:

"If I don't get the boat back, I can't be in the race!"

A moment later his mother was saying, "Hello? This is Mrs. Bobbsey. Will you see if our trunk is down at your office?"

There was silence for nearly five minutes while the girl who had answered the phone went to find out. Bert fumed, and Mrs. Bobbsey nervously tapped one foot as she waited for the answer.

"Hello?" the girl said. "Mrs. Bobbsey, your trunk has already left here."

"Where has it gone?" Bert's mother asked.

"To the railway station, I suppose," the girl said. "Good-bye."

Mrs. Bobbsey turned to Bert and gave him the message. The race he had worked for so hard— now he could not be in it! But a moment later he said excitedly:

"Mother, maybe we can stop the trunk! Come on, let's go to the station!"

He and Mrs. Bobbsey ran out of the house, and jumped into the car. She drove to the railway station, and Bert raced inside. The porter was not in sight, so the boy dashed to the train platform.

There stood a big cart, piled high with trunks, bags, and packages waiting to be put in the luggage van. Bert could hear the locomotive's whistle in the distance. He looked around wildly. Still no sign of the porter.

Bert rushed up to the truck. There was the Bobbsey's trunk! He must get it off!

"What's the matter, son?" a voice behind him asked. "You look mighty excited."

Bert wheeled. What a relief! There stood the porter.

Quickly Bert explained what had happened. The man laughed, and said he was glad Bert had caught the trunk in time. The boy climbed up and helped him shift the various packages and suitcases, until the Bobbsey trunk was uncovered.

By this time Mrs. Bobbsey had come to the platform. Suddenly Bert had an inspiration: maybe the trunk could go after all. He called to his mother, asking if she had the key with her.

"Why, yes, I do," she said, quickly opening her bag and fishing down inside for the key.

The train could be seen coming up the track now.

"Mother, hurry!" Bert cried from his perch on the hand truck.

Mrs. Bobbsey handed him the key. He quickly unlocked the trunk and threw up the lid. Without paying much attention to what would happen to the clothes, he reached down underneath them and pulled out the boat. By this time the train had pulled into the station and was about to stop.

"Hurry!" the porter called. "I can't hold this train up!"

Bert handed the boat to his mother, slammed the lid, and locked the trunk. Then he jumped off the truck, and the man pulled it up to the luggage van.

"Whew! That was a close call!" Bert said in relief.

Mrs. Bobbsey laughed. She never knew what her family was going to do next! But she was very happy that Bert had his boat back. Now he could be in the Saturday race!

CHAPTER XV

WHAT an exciting Saturday morning on Lake
Metoka! The news about the midget motorboat
race had spread, and many people had come by
motorboat and car to see it.

A band was playing on the shore, and boys were
selling popcorn, candy, and balloons.

"It's just like a circus," Flossie exclaimed to her
sister. "Nan, may I have a balloon?"

Nan said she thought they had better wait. If
they wanted to get a good place to watch right
down by the water, they had better not delay. She
had Flossie by one hand, Freddie by the other.

Mr. and Mrs. Bobbsey were coming a little later.
Even Dinah and Sam had decided to leave their
work and watch the race. Everyone wanted to see
how Bert's boat would make out in the race.

A little dock had been built out into the water,
so the contestants could stand on it and attach their
boats to the cable and bridle without wading into

the water. Mr. Warren, who was in charge, was in the water, however, inspecting the pole and the long lines that ran from it. When he was sure everything was in order, he came ashore, and called out through a megaphone:

"Are all the contestants here? If so, report to me."

Fifteen men and boys walked up. In a hat Mr. Warren had several slips of paper with numbers on. The contestants were to draw for places. One by one they put their hands in and pulled out a number.

"What did you get?" Freddie called across to Bert.

"Number twelve," Bert answered.

Mr. Warren asked if number one would please start. A man walked up with a fine-looking midget motorboat. He attached it to the bridle and cable, started its motor, and set it down in the water. It chugged off.

For this race there were two timekeepers. They clicked their watches at the same instant, and then waited for the boat to complete the course. It circled four times. Then, as it started on the last round, the boat came off the bridle and swung around. The man was out of the race!

"That's a shame!" said Nan.

Freddie looked up at her and grinned. "That gives Bert a better chance," he whispered.

As other contestants put their boats into the race, various things happened. One boat tipped over, another stopped in the middle of the race, and still another had a piece come off and jam the motor.

Before Bert knew it, his name was announced to try out the *Rover*. He was a bit nervous, and his hand shook a tiny bit as he fastened the boat to the bridle and cable. He started the motor, and then waited to see what would happen.

The *Rover* zipped around the course at a rate faster than any of the eleven boats before it—at least that was what the timekeepers said when Bert's boat was pulled from the water.

"Hurrah for Bert!" Freddie shouted.

Several people laughed. Then they became silent as contestant number thirteen started his boat. Bert held his breath. At the end, it was found that the time it had taken was a little longer than Bert's. Number fourteen suffered the same fate.

"The last boat will now enter the race!" Mr. Warren called out. "We would appreciate silence, please!"

"I guess he means us," said Freddie, who was jumping up and down and yelling loudly, despite the fact that Nan was trying to keep him quiet.

Freddie did manage to stand very still until the boat finished and Mr. Warren made an announcement.

"According to the stop-watches, there is a tie between Mr. Trent, the last contestant, and Bert Bobbsey. I am going to ask these two contestants to try again. If one boat is faster than the other this time, it will be the winner."

Bert Bobbsey's heart began to pound!

Since Mr. Trent's boat was still attached to the bridle and cable, he went first. Then Bert attached the *Rover* and let it go. The boy was sure it was going faster than the other boat, but the stop-watches would tell the result. After the *Rover* had gone around five times, he took it from the water.

There were a few seconds of silence, as Mr. Warren and the two timekeepers conferred. Then Mr. Warren, turning towards the watchers on shore, smiled and said:

"By only two-tenths of a second Bert Bobbsey is the winner!"

"Wheeeeeeeeeeeeeee!" cried Freddie and Flossie together and ran around excitedly.

Mr. Trent, the loser, and several other people came to shake hands with Bert. They told him his boat was not only speedy but very fine looking. Mr. Warren clapped for silence, and then said to the people standing around:

"As you may have heard, the winner of this race is entitled to go to Whitesail Harbour and compete in the Interstate Races. I'm glad to announce that Bert Bobbsey is going to."

Everyone clapped loudly—so loudly, in fact, that Bert blushed. But he was very happy. Now he could go into the big race!

After most of the people had left, Mr. Warren

came up to Mr. and Mrs. Bobbsey and congratulated them also. Then he said he would like to give Bert and his family a special prize. They all waited expectantly to hear what it was.

"It isn't anything you can see," he said mysteriously. "I have an uncle whose name is Captain Windy. He owns a large clipper ship which I understand he is sailing across the bay to Whitesail Harbour.

"I spoke to him on the telephone last night and asked him if he would permit you people to take your car on board instead of going all the way by road."

"That would be wonderful!" Nan was the first to speak up.

"I agree with my daughter," Mrs. Bobbsey smiled.

The twins' father said that this was a mighty fine offer indeed. He did not see how he could refuse it, and he was certainly grateful for the chance to show his children what a clipper ship looked like.

Mr. Warren smiled at the twins and said, "There's a mystery in connection with this clipper ship. I'm not going to tell you what it is. You'll have to find out for yourselves."

The rest of that day and for a few days after, the twins made all kinds of guesses what the mystery of the clipper ship might be. Flossie was sure it was a ghost. Nan thought maybe it was a treasure. Freddie thought it might be a special kind of fire apparatus, and Bert was sure the clipper carried some special kind of sail.

"It won't be long before we'll find out," said Mr. Bobbsey one evening. "Your mother and I have decided we'll start in the morning."

There was hustle and bustle in the Bobbsey household after breakfast as last-minute things were packed. Flossie put her doll in the car. Freddie carried out his tank of goldfish safely wedged in the crate. Bert, who had made a fine cover for the *Rover*, placed his boat above the back seat.

"All aboard!" Mr. Bobbsey called out at nine o'clock.

One by one the family climbed into the car. Mr. Bobbsey was in the driver's seat with Freddie and Bert beside him. Mrs. Bobbsey and the two girls sat in the back.

After everyone was seated, and the doors were closed, Dinah, Sam, and Waggo came outside. The little dog barked furiously and jumped around. Then he began to do some of his tricks, somersaulting, sitting up and begging, and barking shrilly.

"He's so cute, I hate to leave him," Flossie remarked, and called out, "We won't be gone long, Waggo."

Dinah and Sam waved as the car moved off, and the couple soon were out of sight. Mr. Bobbsey drove until noontime. Then he stopped at a cool spot in the woods where they ate the lunch Dinah had packed. Then they started off again.

An hour later they came to the sea-shore, and began their hunt for the clipper ship. None of the children had guessed what the mystery was, and when they found the ship, the children jumped from the car and hurried up the gang-plank.

Standing on the deck was a fine old gentleman with white hair and a white beard. They were

sure from his suit and cap that he was the owner of the boat.

"You're Captain Windy, aren't you?" Freddie asked, and he nodded.

"Welcome, little people." He smiled at the small twins.

Then he shook hands with Nan and Bert, and said he was glad to see them. By this time Mrs. Bobbsey had come up the gang-plank, and spoke to him. She said Mr. Bobbsey was waiting to hear how he was to put the car on board. She would go and tell him.

"We have a special gang-plank," the captain said. "I'll see about it in a few minutes."

As soon as Flossie and Freddie felt they had stayed talking to Captain Windy long enough to be polite, they hurried through a doorway into the cabin of the clipper ship. To their amazement there were tanks of fish built into the walls.

"Oh, aren't they funny-looking fish!" Flossie said, and hurried over to look at some which were called sea-horses.

"Do you suppose this is the mystery?" Freddie asked her.

His twin said she did not know. "Let's go out on deck and see if there is some mystery there," Flossie suggested.

A few minutes later they did find another mystery. There was a long, deep tank built into the deck of the boat. As the children looked into it, they saw a large animal swimming around.

"What's that?" Freddie asked Bert, who had come up to look.

"It's a porpoise," Bert answered.

Freddie wanted to see it better. He stepped up on a ledge and leaned far over. The next moment he lost his balance and went head first down into the porpoise tank!

CHAPTER XVI

HO-HO, THE PORPOISE

"DAD! Captain Windy!" shouted Bert.

Neither of the men heard the cry, because in his excitement Bert was calling down into the tank where Freddie had fallen. Nan heard, though, and ran over to see what was the matter.

To the amazement of the older twins the porpoise was not hurting Freddie. Instead, it was frisking about the little boy, who could swim enough to stay on top of the water.

"The porpoise is playing with Freddie!" Bert exclaimed in wonder.

"Just the same, we have to get him out of there," Nan said, worried.

She ran to find Captain Windy. He laughed when he heard what had happened and Nan was surprised that he did not seem alarmed.

"Why, Ho-Ho wouldn't hurt anybody," he said.

As he reached the tank, the captain explained that Ho-Ho was the name of the porpoise. And what a good name it was, because Ho-Ho seemed to be having a lot of fun. First, the roly-poly sea animal would dive down deep under Freddie, then suddenly leap out of the water and over the little boy's head. Of course, this made waves, and frightened Freddie dreadfully.

"I don't think Freddie wants to play," Nan insisted.

"Maybe not," said Captain Windy.

He picked up a coil of rope and flung it over the side of the tank.

"Catch hold, Freddie!" he ordered.

The older twins held their breath. Was their little brother too scared to do what he was told? For a few seconds it looked as if this might be the case, because the porpoise, not understanding, wanted to continue playing. He kept bumping into the rope, so that Freddie could not reach it.

"I'm going down there and get Freddie!" said Bert suddenly, and climbed to the edge of the tank.

Captain Windy caught Bert's shoulder, and told him not to. Then in a loud voice he called, "Ho-Ho! Stop bothering the little boy!"

Obeying his master, the porpoise finished the dive he was making and then lay still. But he was not through teasing. Unexpectedly he shot a stream of water into the air, sending the spray over the captain and the older twins.

"Catch hold of the rope!" the captain ordered Freddie.

This time the little boy was able to catch it.

Captain Windy pulled it up slowly, hoping that Freddie could hold on tightly. Fortunately, Freddie had often practised being a fireman, and he knew exactly how to twist the rope around his arms so that he could not lose it.

As soon as poor Freddie reached the deck, he began to cry. Nan put her arms around him, saying he was all right, and the porpoise was only playing.

Freddie wiped away his tears, then he said, "But I'm all wet. What'll I do?"

Nan said she would run to the car to speak to her mother. When Mrs. Bobbsey heard what had happened, she shook her head, and wondered what was going to happen next. Mr. Bobbsey opened the back of the car and took out one of the suitcases, in which were some of Freddie's clothes.

As soon as the little boy had changed into dry clothing, Captain Windy showed the Bobbseys around the ship. On the deck was another tank of fish, which he said were named Plaice.

"I call these my backward fish," he said with a smile. "Most fish are dark on the back and white on the stomach. Plaice are just the other way around."

The captain said the strange fish could change colour wherever they wanted to, and make themselves look like seaweed. In this way they fooled other fish which wanted to eat them.

"And they don't lie on their backs either," the captain added. "They lie on one side."

"Which way do they swim?" Bert asked.

The captain said the fish could swim almost any way they wanted to. That depended on where they were. When they were lying still, they were often found on their sides.

All this time he had been prodding around in the tank with a pole, trying to make the fish come to the surface. When this failed, he took a small bell on a rope from his pocket, and lowered it into the water. As soon as he shook it, several fish came to the surface.

Flossie laughed. "Is that the way you call them to dinner?"

"Yes, it is," the captain answered.

The children had never seen such strange fish. Both their eyes were on the right side of their heads, and their mouths were twisted in queer, lopsided fashion.

"Why do they have such funny eyes and mouths?" Freddie asked.

The captain explained that a Plaice likes to twist and turn its eyes about in all directions. Sometimes it wants to look up through the water, sometimes in front of it, sometimes behind, sometimes on one side or the other. Then it can be sure to spot an enemy.

"The funny thing about it," the captain said, "is that the baby fish are not born looking like their parents. The little ones have straight mouths and one eye on each side of their heads.

"But soon something very strange happens. The left eye of the baby fish begins to move slowly up across its head. After a while it lands on the other side, and there it stays."

"When does its mouth get crooked?" Flossie wanted to know.

The captain told her that as the eye began to travel, the mouth began to get crooked. It was not long before the little fish looked exactly like its mother and father.

"Have you any more funny-looking fish on board?" Freddie asked, remembering the aquarium he had seen in the cabin.

Captain Windy said he would have to show them the other fish later. It was time to set sail. He called to three of his crew and told them to make ready. His eyes twinkling, Captain Windy began to tease the children by speaking in strange terms to his crew.

"Better pull down Blue Peter," he said.

The twins stared. Who could Blue Peter be? Moreover, it was not very nice to pull him down. They said nothing, however, and a few moments later laughed as the sailor brought down a small blue flag with a square white centre, which had been flying to let people know the clipper would be sailing within twenty-four hours.

"Well, if you children will excuse me," Captain Windy said, "I believe I'll go afterbody."

The twins' eyes popped. Then they thought he might be teasing them again. The old sea captain walked towards the back of the clipper, and one of the crew whispered that on a ship the rear section of the vessel is sometimes called the afterbody.

Mr. Bobbsey drove his car aboard, up a special, wide gang-plank, and in a few minutes the crew hoisted several sails and they set out across the harbour. All four children stuck close to Captain Windy. They liked him very much, and hoped he would use more of his funny expressions. Presently, seeing Freddie yawn, he asked:

"Would you like a donkey's breakfast?"

The twins howled with laughter, and asked what a donkey's breakfast was. The captain told them they must guess. They guessed wheat and oats and hay, but Captain Windy said on shipboard a donkey's breakfast is something quite different.

"Please tell us," Flossie begged.

"It's a sailor's mattress with a straw filling," he answered.

Presently he became serious, and told them that this clipper had made a fine record winning races years before. Now it was too old and had to stay in the bay.

"But she's still good and seaworthy, and I've turned her into a marine museum," he said. "When I tie up on shore, I charge admission for people to see my strange fish. That's how I earn a living."

"Do you live on the clipper ship all the time— sleep here, too?" Nan asked.

Captain Windy nodded. He said that once in a while he went to visit his sister who lived at Whitesail Harbour.

"Her name is Miss Evy Brett, but everyone calls her Miss Windy. She runs a gift shop right on the beach," he told them. "I'm sure you twins would like to go and visit it. She has all sorts of curious articles to sell."

Nan asked where the articles came from. Captain Windy said that a great many of them were brought to his sister by beachcombers. Turning to the small twins, he asked:

"Do you know what a beachcomber is?"

To his surprise the small twins did. They had been to the seaside one summer visiting their aunt and uncle, and they had learned that a beachcomber was a man who walked up and down the beach gathering things which were swept in by the waves.

"My sister can tell you a lot of interesting stories about Whitesail Harbour," the old man said. "Years ago there were some shipwrecks off the shore, and every once in a while something valuable is found buried in the sand there."

"Really?" the twins said, their eyes shining.

"Yes, indeed," Captain Windy said. "Maybe while you're walking along the beach, you'll find a treasure yourself."

CHAPTER XVII

AT WHITESAIL HARBOUR

"LOOK at all those boats with white sails!" Flossie said to her twin, as they leaned on the rail looking towards Whitesail Harbour.

"But none of them has as many sails as we have," Freddie replied staunchly. He already was fond of the old clipper ship.

Mr. Bobbsey walked over to the children, pointing to the sandy beach, which was just coming into view.

"See that long, white building over there?" he asked them. "That's the hotel where we're going to stay."

"It's right on the beach!" Freddie said excitedly. "We can go straight out of the door into the water."

All the Bobbseys gathered to watch the shore-line grow bigger, as the clipper neared it. Presently Captain Windy ordered some of the sails reefed, and after a while they glided up to a pier.

As soon as the ship was moored with her sails

down, Mr. Bobbsey drove the car off the boat. His family followed, all waving good-bye, and saying they would come soon again to see Captain Windy. There had not been enough time for him to explain about all the strange fish on his museum ship.

It was nearly supper-time, but there was about half an hour left for the children to watch the very small sailboats come in. Nan declared she had never seen a prettier sight, with the setting sun making a wavering red streak across the water.

When Bert and Freddie finally got to their room, Bert decided that he had better put the *Rover* in a safe place. He was sure no one would steal it, but he was afraid that someone might tinker with the motor. It was in good shape, and he did not want anything to happen before the big race. He finally decided to put the *Rover* in the bottom drawer of the bureau.

"Freddie," he said, "will you promise not to touch this boat?"

His brother looked a little hurt. Of course he would not touch the valuable boat. Didn't he want Bert to win the race?

After breakfast next morning Mr. Bobbsey drove off to attend to the business which had brought him to Whitesail Harbour. As soon as he had gone, Bert went up to the hotel desk and inquired about boys' camps near by.

"There's only one," the clerk answered, "so you must mean Pine Trail Camp."

"Can you tell me how to get to it?" Bert asked.

The man gave him simple directions. If Bert would walk to the main part of town and take a bus along the beach road one mile, then walk towards the ocean, he would come to it. While the desk clerk was speaking, one of the hotel guests stopped to get his mail. Hearing the conversation, he said to Bert:

"I'm going to drive out to Pine Trail Camp this morning. I have a son staying there. Would you like to go with me and my wife?"

"Why, yes, sir. Thank you," Bert said, smiling. "I'll ask Mother."

The man, who said his name was Mr. Strong, asked if Bert would like to take anyone with him. Bert introduced himself, mentioning that he had a twin and that he had a younger brother and sister who were twins also. Maybe one or all of them might like to go.

"I'd be very glad to take you all," Mr. Strong said. "I've never had the honour of carrying two sets of twins in my car at once."

Bert hurried away to speak to his mother, who was looking at a display of rare ferns in the corner of the lobby. She said that it would be very nice for the twins to go to the camp, but that she and Nan and Flossie had planned to go to the curio and gift shop owned by Captain Windy's sister. She did not know whether Freddie would like to go with them, or with Bert. Would Bert find out? Freddie was in his room.

"We're not going until half-past ten," said Mrs. Bobbsey. "When are you going?"

Bert ran back to ask Mr. Strong, who said they would start from the rear entrance of the hotel at quarter-past ten. Bert went to his room and found Freddie putting on his bathing suit.

"I'm going out and dig treasure," the little boy said. "Why don't you come with me, Bert?"

"Because I'm going to Danny Rugg's camp and talk to him," Bert answered. "Wouldn't you like to come with me?"

Freddie did not know what to do. He wanted to dig for treasure. He wanted to go with his mother and Nan and Flossie to see the unusual things in the curio shop. He also wanted to go with Bert.

"Tell you what I'll do," he said. "If I decide to go with you, Bert, I'll meet you when it's time to go."

"Okay. If you want to go to the camp, be at the back entrance of the hotel at quarter-past ten *sharp*," Bert told him.

Freddie promised, although he said if he got busy hunting for treasure, he would not come.

"I can tell when it's quarter-past ten," he said. "I saw a big clock up in that tower on the hotel. I guess they put it there for children on the beach."

Bert went off, and at quarter-past ten was on hand to meet Mr. and Mrs. Strong. When he said his small brother might come too, they waited five minutes. Since Freddie did not appear, Bert said Freddie probably was going with his mother to the curio shop. Bert was sure Mrs. Bobbsey would not leave Freddie alone on the beach.

When they reached Pine Trail Camp, Bert jumped out of the car and opened the door for Mrs. Strong.

"I know a boy who is staying here at the camp, and I'd like to go to see him," Bert said. "Will that be all right?"

"Sure, son. We'll stay here until noontime," Mr. Strong answered. "Suppose we say we'll meet you at the car at quarter to twelve."

Bert promised to be there. He went off in search of Danny. Bert had no special plan for finding out if the mean boy had the stolen *Challenger*, but as he walked along the water front, he saw a group of boys in swimming. One of them was Danny.

"That's good," Bert thought. "Now I can find where his tent is and look around without his knowing it."

Meeting another swimmer on his way to the beach, Bert asked him where Danny Rugg lived. The boy pointed to a big cabin near a sand dune and asked Bert if he would like to visit it. Bert said he would, and together he and the boy walked towards it.

"What's your name?" Bert asked.

"Ken Strong. What's yours?"

Bert told him and then asked if Mr. Strong was his father. When the boy replied that he was, Bert told Ken that his parents probably were looking for him.

Hearing this, Ken quickly led Bert into the cabin, and, excusing himself, said:

"Look around all you please. I'm going to find Mother and Dad."

Bert thanked him and looked through the cabin, but there was no way of telling which was Danny's cot. There was no sign of a motorboat.

"Maybe I'd better look under the cots," he told himself.

Getting down on his hands and knees, Bert peered under every cot. There were suitcases, heavy trunks, games, books, and athletic equipment—but no boats. Straightening up, Bert said to himself:

"Well, the missing boat isn't here. If Danny has the *Challenger*, it must be somewhere else."

At this moment a young man walked in, and Bert introduced himself, saying he knew Danny Rugg in Lakeport. He asked the man, who was the supervisor, if the boy had brought a speed-boat to camp.

"I really don't know," the man replied. "Why don't you run down to the shore front and ask Danny?"

Bert did not want to say that he hoped to avoid Danny if possible. He hurried from the cabin, and upon meeting another boy, asked where model boats that had been brought to camp would be kept.

"There are some down in the boathouse," the other boy told Bert, and pointed out the building. "Is there any special boat you want to see?"

Bert did not know whether it was wise to mention Danny's boat or not, but he decided he might as well find out. To his surprise, the boy replied that he had not seen Danny's boat but that he had bragged about a wonderful one he had brought, which he was going to enter in the big race.

Bert's heart almost stopped beating. He was sure that it must be the missing *Challenger*!

"Thanks a lot!" he said, and hurried down the trail towards the boathouse. He nearly reached it, when he heard a voice say:

"What are you doing here?"

Bert turned to see Danny Rugg and two other boys almost upon him. Before he could answer or jump aside to avoid trouble, they began to fight him.

"I'll teach you to spy on me!" Danny cried furiously. "How did you get to Whitesail Harbour, anyhow? I'll bet you came just to make trouble for me!"

It was an uneven fight, and Bert was getting the worst of it, when another camper rushed up.

"Hey! Cut it out, you fellers!" he cried. "The supervisor is coming!"

Danny and his friends gave Bert a hard shove, sending him down into a deep gully. Then they hustled off towards the beach.

Bert lay dazed for several seconds. Then he tried to get up. As he stepped on one foot, his ankle turned under him, and he cried out in pain. He sat down for a few minutes, then tried again.

It was no use. Something had happened to Bert's ankle. He could not walk!

CHAPTER XVIII

THE CURIO SHOP

BERT slowly dragged himself out of the gully. Reaching the top, he saw a young man coming, and waved to him.

"Will you please help me?" he called. "I've hurt my ankle."

The young man was a supervisor by the name of Drake, but the boys called him Doc, because he was in medical school. He sat down on the ground beside Bert and examined his ankle.

"It's not sprained," he said. "But it has a bad bruise on the bone. It'll probably hurt you for a few days."

"Will it be all right to walk on it?" Bert asked.

Doc said it would hurt, but it would not do the ankle any harm.

"Are you one of the campers?" he asked, seeing that Bert did not wear the camp uniform.

"No, I'm not," Bert said. "I came over here with Mr. and Mrs. Strong."

Bert would have liked to mention Danny Rugg and tell of the mean trick he had played, but he kept quiet. Doc Drake helped him to the beach, where Mr. and Mrs. Strong were watching their son swim. Seeing Bert limp, they were concerned, but he assured them nothing much was the matter.

"We hear you and Ken have already met each other," Mrs. Strong said. "I'm sure you will be friends."

When their son came out of the water, he invited Bert to go up to his cabin while he dressed.

"I can't walk very well," Bert said sadly. "I—I fell into the gully and hurt my ankle."

Ken hurried off and came back in a few minutes wearing his camp uniform. Then he and Bert began to talk.

Presently Bert told him he knew Danny Rugg, and wondered if he had brought a boat to camp. "He wouldn't tell me in Lakeport," Bert added.

"I'm not exactly a friend of Danny's," Ken said, "but I'll find out and let you know."

In a few minutes a bugle sounded. Ken said this was the call to lunch. He was sorry Bert and his parents could not stay, but this was not visitors' day. Perhaps they could come another time.

"I'd sure like to," said Bert. "This is a grand camp."

When he got back to the hotel with Mr. and Mrs. Strong, Bert did not see any of his family around, and supposed they were not back yet from the curio shop. This was true. At half-past ten that morning Mrs. Bobbsey, Nan, and Flossie had left the hotel. They had looked for Freddie, but not seeing him they had assumed he had gone with Bert.

After walking along the beach for some distance they reached the shop. Captain Windy's sister proved to be a delightful elderly woman, who had twinkling blue eyes like her brother. She was very interested to hear that the Bobbseys had come across the bay to Whitesail Harbour in the clipper ship.

After Flossie had looked around a few minutes, she said, "This is the most be-yootiful store I've ever seen!"

Miss Windy laughed, saying she did not know how beautiful the shop was. She did think it had many rare articles for sale.

"Right now I haven't so many things as usual," she said. "Drifty, my beachcomber, hasn't been here for over a week. I depend on him to bring me things he finds on the beach, and also to help in the shop."

"Why hasn't he come?" Flossie asked.

Miss Windy said she had no idea, but she was afraid the old man might be ill. Unfortunately she could not find out about him, because no one seemed to know where he lived.

"He lives in a little hut somewhere up the beach, but he has always kept it a secret." Then she added, "After you look around, I'll show you the back room where I make rugs."

"Oh, may I see them now?" Nan asked, and told her about the rug-making class in Lakeport.

"A fine thing for girls to learn," Miss Windy said approvingly. "I've been making rugs for many years, ever since I was a lass like you. People from all over send me orders. Right now I have an order for a set of three rugs to be exactly alike but in different sizes."

"How nice," Nan said.

"But I don't know how I can ever finish them," Miss Windy continued sadly. "They are a wedding present, and there's not much time left for me to deliver them."

"Maybe Freddie and I could keep shop for you while you work," Flossie offered. She explained that Freddie was her twin brother, who had gone off to visit a camp with Nan's twin.

"That's very kind of you, my dear," Miss Windy answered. "If I get into trouble here, I'll let you know."

Nan had been looking at a pile of rags in a corner. The colours were very beautiful, and she wondered which ones Miss Windy was going to use for the wedding rugs. Finally she asked her.

Miss Windy picked out several. She said the yellow, white, and pale blue were to go together. Pink, pale grey, and light purple were to come next.

At this moment a customer came into the shop, and Miss Windy hurried outside to wait on her. While she was gone, Nan fingered the various pieces to be plaited.

"Maybe I could help Miss Windy right now by plaiting some of these for her," she thought. "Her brother was so nice to give us a ride on the clipper. I ought to do something to help the Windy family."

Nan decided not to make the mistake Freddie had made by cutting off any of the pieces. She picked up strips of yellow, white, and pale blue, and pinned them on to a board she saw. Quickly she pulled the strips taut, and made a very good-looking plait. Then she started another of the next colour.

All this time Mrs. Bobbsey and Flossie had been looking around the shop. Flossie had spied a cunning doll made of shells, and wanted to buy it. Mrs. Bobbsey finally consented.

Then she herself saw a piece of strangely shaped driftwood. It looked like a long dachshund. Flossie giggled, declaring that from where she stood, it really could be a dog.

"Please let's buy it and fool people," the little girl pleaded.

Mrs. Bobbsey said that it was too expensive to buy just for a joke. She thought, however, it might make a very unusual holder for flower and fern arrangements. Miss Windy told her that certain kinds of fern from Whitesail Harbour would grow readily in pockets of the driftwood, so Mrs. Bobbsey purchased the "dachshund".

At this moment Miss Windy realized that Nan was still in the back room and went to speak to her. Mrs. Bobbsey and Flossie followed. To their amazement Nan had several plaits ready to be sewed into the wedding gift rug.

"Why, bless you, my child!" Miss Windy exclaimed. "Why, they are beautifully done! When you told me you had gone to a rug-making class, I had no idea you could plait so well."

Proudly Flossie spoke up, saying a picture of her sister's rug had been in the paper. And Dinah had said she liked it because it had a piece of all the Bobbsey family in it. Miss Windy laughed, and had to be told the story of Nan's birthday gift to Dinah.

"That was very thoughtful of you," the shop owner said. Then, looking intently at Nan, she added, "If your mother would let you do it, I wish you would come and help me with my big order."

Mrs. Bobbsey hardly knew what to say. Knowing Nan, she felt that her daughter would want to help Miss Windy. On the other hand, they were not to be at Whitesail Harbour for long, and Nan really should be outdoors playing on the beach rather than working indoors.

"Thank you very much, Miss Windy," the twins' mother said. "Shall we leave it this way? If you find that you really do need Nan, I shall be glad to let her come for about an hour each day. Would that be all right?"

Miss Windy said this would be a great help. She would let the Bobbseys know if she was getting too far behind in her work.

"It all depends on Drifty," she said. "He may

come back at any time, but if he doesn't, I really will need some other help."

On the way back to the hotel Nan kept thinking about the curio shop and the beachcomber who had not shown up for several days. He probably was ill in his cabin with no one there to help him or bring him food. Turning to her mother, she said:

"This afternoon I'd like to go with Bert and hunt for Drifty. Would that be all right?"

Mrs. Bobbsey said she assumed it would be. But she would inquire of the hotel clerk approximately where the place was, and whether it would be safe for the children to go up the beach alone.

CHAPTER XIX

FLOSSIE'S GREAT SEARCH

PROMISING that she and Bert would not go too far from the beach in their hunt for Drifty's cabin, Nan hurried ahead of her mother and Flossie to find Bert.

To her amazement he was seated in a beach chair in the garden of the hotel. This was not like Bert, and Nan knew at once that something had happened. Learning about his injured ankle, she wanted to know all the details.

By this time Mrs. Bobbsey and Flossie arrived. They too heard the story, and Flossie declared:

"They ought to make Danny go home from that camp!"

Bert smiled, saying that if Danny went home, the Bobbseys would have to worry about him in Lakeport. It would be better if Danny could stay away for the whole summer. Flossie agreed. Then a moment later she asked:

"Did you and Freddie have fun at the camp before you hurt your ankle?"

"Freddie didn't go to the camp with me," Bert answered, surprised.

Mrs. Bobbsey, who was examining Bert's swollen ankle, looked up in alarm. "Freddie didn't go to camp with you?"

Then the story came out. Freddie had not gone with Bert, and he had not gone with the others either. Then where was he?

"Flossie," said Mrs. Bobbsey, "go up to Freddie's room and see if he's there."

Flossie ran off, took the lift, and raced down the hall to Freddie's bedroom. The door was not locked, so she walked in. Her twin was not there. Thinking he might have heard her coming and be hiding, she called out:

"Freddie, if you're here, don't play tricks. It's serious. Nobody knows where you are!"

She waited a couple of seconds. When there was no answer, she was sure Freddie was not hiding. She raced back to the garden to report to the others.

"I'll inquire at the desk and see if the clerk knows where Freddie is," Mrs. Bobbsey said, a worried look coming over her face.

The man claimed he had not seen Freddie since breakfast-time. Mrs. Bobbsey now asked several of the hotel guests, and Nan, too, inquired for her small brother. No one had seen Freddie.

"The last time I saw him he was putting on his

bathing suit," said Bert, when his mother and sisters came back to where he was sitting. "Freddie said he was going out to the beach to dig treasure."

Suddenly Flossie burst into tears. "My twin— maybe he was eaten up by a big fish!"

"Don't say such things!" Nan told her little sister.

The Bobbseys were extremely worried, but the twins' mother tried to remain calm about the situation. She suggested that they walk among the bathers and inquire if any of them had seen Freddie. Fifteen minutes later they returned to Bert again, with no word of the missing boy.

"Even if my ankle hurts, I'm going to hunt for Freddie," Bert declared.

"Don't do that," Mrs. Bobbsey urged him. "I feel sure that if Freddie had been in trouble along the beach, someone would have seen him. There are lifeguards watching, you know."

Flossie dried her eyes. Suddenly she had an idea about where her brother might be. The evening before, Freddie had said his goldfish needed more food. Flossie was sure he had gone to a pet shop to buy some.

"I'll bet Freddie got lost on his way," she said, "and maybe he's in the police station."

Her mother replied that Freddie most certainly knew his name and the name of the hotel where he was staying. If the police had him, they would have brought him back.

"Perhaps he went down the beach to find food

for his fish," Bert suggested. "He told me that a man in the hotel said goldfish liked to eat ground-up crab meat. Maybe Freddie went to find baby crabs."

"Ooo-eee!" Flossie cried. "Maybe a big crab got him, and hurt him, and he can't get home!"

"Flossie, you can think of the most dreadful things!" Nan said. "Why don't you think hard about where Freddie might be?"

Flossie looked hurt. She said she had thought of more places than anybody else. Mrs. Bobbsey hugged her little daughter and said indeed she was trying very hard to find Freddie. She herself was going far down the beach to see if by chance Freddie was looking for food for his goldfish. She would take Flossie with her, while Nan went in the other direction.

Bert felt bad that he could not go, but when he stepped on his foot, he winced in pain. Since he wanted to be in the midget speedboat race, he concluded it would be better to sit still and not aggravate the soreness in the ankle bone.

By this time several people who had overheard the Bobbseys talking offered to hunt for Freddie also. They started off in various directions, but when they returned about twenty minutes later, not one of them had any news of the missing child. The Bobbseys had no better luck.

Not knowing what else to do, Mrs. Bobbsey telephoned to the police station. The sergeant in charge said they would start a search for the little boy at once. The officer asked several questions—

what Freddie liked to do and what he might have wanted to see.

Mrs. Bobbsey at once thought of Freddie's love of fire engines, and said perhaps her small son had gone to the town firestation. He also liked to play detective, and possibly he was off with some policeman. The sergeant promised to start an immediate hunt for the little boy.

Flossie had been listening to the telephone conversation. When she heard her mother say that Freddie liked to play fireman and detective, the little girl began to think of other things Freddie liked to do. He liked to go fishing. He loved to ride. Maybe he had found a pony some place and was having fun with it.

"I believe you children should have some lunch," Mrs. Bobbsey told Flossie, and they returned to Bert and Nan in the garden.

Luncheon was being served by several waiters, and the children took the little trays which were offered to them. But none of them felt like eating. They were too eager to hear from the police about Freddie.

"I'm going to my room," Flossie told her mother, and skipped off.

The truth was that Flossie wanted to cry. There was no one in the whole world who loved Freddie the way she did, she was sure. She *must* find him! Flossie had a feeling that if she could just cry for a little while, maybe it would clear her mind, and she could figure out where her twin was.

After about ten minutes, Flossie dried her eyes, washed her face, and looked into the mirror as she combed her hair. In the glass was reflected a picture hanging on the wall behind her. It was the picture of a clipper ship.

Flossie stared at it as if she had seen a ghost. Suddenly she put down the comb she was using, rushed from the room, and raced all the way downstairs without waiting for the lift.

The little girl started for the spot where she had left her family. Then she changed her mind. She had been wrong several times about where Freddie might be. This time she was going to investigate all by herself!

Half running, half skipping, Flossie headed for Captain Windy's clipper ship. She felt sure Freddie was there. Hurrying up the gang-plank, she thought she heard a small boy's voice. Was it her twin's?

"Now, ladies and gentlemen," the young voice was saying, "I once fell into this porpoise tank!"

Flossie's fears were over. She burst out laughing. Her little brother had taken on the job of amusing sightseers by telling the story of what had happened to him.

Running to the forward part of the ship, the little girl saw quite a crowd of people standing near the tank. Several of them were laughing.

"You don't mean to say you actually fell into that tank and the porpoise didn't hurt you?" a boy called out.

Freddie insisted that was exactly what had happened. As a matter of fact, the porpoise had wanted to play with him.

Flossie was almost afraid that Freddie would dive in again just to prove it. But the little boy went on to say:

"Now if you'll follow me into the cabin, I'll tell you about the fish in there. Wait until you see the sea-horse!"

As Freddie stepped in front of the sightseers and led the way to the cabin, Flossie ran up to him.

"Freddie, we're all so worried about you. Why didn't you say you were coming here?"

Freddie stood up as tall as he was able to, and looked at his little sister, a very annoyed expression on his face.

"Don't bother me just now," he said. "I have business to attend to."

CHAPTER XX

THE BEACHCOMBER

WHEN Flossie saw that Freddie was not going to listen to her and go back to the hotel, she decided to find Captain Windy. He was sitting in a little office, talking to two of his crew.

" 'Scuse me, Captain Windy," Flossie cried, "but I have something very important to tell you."

The skipper turned and smiled at the little girl, asking her what it was.

"Freddie's been lost from us and everybody's worried," she said. "But he won't come home. Please make him go."

Captain Windy puckered his brows. "You mean you didn't know where Freddie was?"

Now it was Flossie's turn to look surprised. She said of course not, and she had finally worked out where her twin might be. When the captain heard this, he jumped up and went outside to where Freddie was still talking to the sightseers. He leaned down and whispered to him.

"All right, Captain Windy, if you say so," Flossie heard Freddie reply. "But may I come again some time and have chow with you?" Freddie had to explain that this meant food on shipboard.

The Captain smiled and said yes, Freddie might come again, but next time he must ask his parents' permission. The twins said good-bye and hurried off.

"We had a good lunch on the clipper," Freddie told his twin, as they walked back to the hotel. "We had clipper soup, and clipper sandwiches, and clipper pudding."

Flossie wanted to know what these were. Freddie said the soup was black bean soup, and the sandwiches corned beef. "The dessert was plum duff," he concluded.

"What's that?" Flossie asked.

Freddie felt pretty important that he had learned several sea terms during the morning. He said plum duff was sailor's pudding made out of flour and water and raisins.

The rest of the Bobbsey family was mighty glad to see Freddie. When he told them that he had been helping Captain Windy, they agreed that this was a nice thing to do. Only of course, he should have told someone where he was going. Freddie was surprised to learn that Bert had thought he had gone with his mother, and that his mother had thought he had gone to camp with Bert.

"Did you find Danny Rugg and the *Challenger?*" Freddie asked his brother.

Bert told him he had found Danny but not Mr. Warren's missing boat. Suddenly Freddie noticed Bert's swollen ankle, and asked what had happened. When he heard that Danny was responsible for it, the little boy said he would like to go right out to the camp and give Danny a good punch.

Next morning Bert's ankle felt better. Although he was not allowed to walk on it for very long at a time, it felt well enough for him to go to the racing headquarters and enter his boat in the contest. Mr. Strong drove him to the beach-front office.

Bert gave his name, and a letter he had brought from Mr. Warren. Seeing the *Rover,* the official said it was a fine craft and when Bert told him he had made it, the man looked very surprised.

"It certainly is speedy looking," he said. "Let's see it in action."

The man had a pole, bridle, and cable in the water, and Bert attached his midget motorboat to it. Then he clicked a little lever and off went the *Rover.* After it had gone around several times, with the man clocking it, he said it surely was a good boat.

"In the big race here," the official told Bert, "you understand we will not use the bridle and cable. There will be a regular course. This makes the race more difficult. The boats have be adjusted to the movement of the water and to the wind."

"Yes, I know," Bert replied. "Mr. Warren told me that."

The man said the course would be marked out two days later, and the contestants could try out their boats. Bert said he would be on hand to test the *Rover*.

During the afternoon the boy polished his boat so that it gleamed beautifully. Then he started the motor and listened carefully. It was purring smoothly.

After breakfast next day, Mrs. Bobbsey suggested that all the children go to the beach early. It was a beautiful day, and they had not played in the sand very much. Soon Freddie and Flossie were in their bathing suits and making a cave near the water.

"Bert," his mother said, "I believe it might help your ankle to walk in the water. Why don't you try it?"

He did, and in a few minutes said that the ankle felt better. Then Bert suggested to Nan that they walk down the beach to the curio shop. He had not been there, and his sister's description of the place intrigued him.

Upon reaching the shop, Bert found the place all that Nan had said. Forgetting about his ankle, Bert wandered around, looking at all the strange gifts that Miss Windy had for sale.

When Miss Windy came from the rug room,

Nan introduced her brother, then said, "You have many new things here. Has Drifty come back?"

"No, he hasn't," Miss Windy replied. "I was getting so low on things, I decided to go out and hunt for some myself. I was fortunate to find several interesting articles to sell."

"But how about your wedding rugs?" Nan asked.

Miss Windy admitted that she had not worked on them much. She had had many visitors to the shop, and between waiting on them and hunting for curios, she had little time for rug making.

At once Nan offered to help with the rugs. She thought Bert should rest his ankle anyway before he walked any farther.

The twins remained for an hour. In that time Nan plaited strips and sewed them on, completing one of the rugs. Miss Windy was very grateful. "I believe I'll be able to deliver the wedding gift after all!" she said, smiling.

As the children left the shop, Bert declared that his ankle felt almost well. "Why don't we go down the beach and see if we can find Drifty's cabin?" he suggested.

"I think it's a grand idea," Nan replied, and the two set off.

For some distance along the beach there were shops and cottages which belonged to summer residents. But presently the houses grew fewer, and after a while there were none at all. Now, the sand, instead of being flat, was heaped here and there into great dunes. Tall grass grew upon them.

"It would be easy to hide a hut behind these dunes," Nan declared excitedly. "Maybe Drifty's cabin is nearby!"

Instead of walking along the shoreline, she and Bert turned inland, zigzagging among the dunes. This took a great deal of time, and for a while they saw no sign of a hut.

Then suddenly Bert spied a little cabin. The twins walked to it and knocked. A kindly old woman came to the door.

"Do you know where Drifty lives?" Nan asked her.

The woman said she had never heard of Drifty.

When Nan explained that he was a beachcomber, who took curios to Miss Windy's shop, the woman said she had heard of a mysterious man, who lived way up the beach. "But it's much too far and desolate for you children to go there alone," she added.

"Thank you, we won't," said Nan, and the children turned away.

They were disappointed, but realized they had already come a long way. When Nan looked at her wrist watch, she said it was lunchtime—they must return to the hotel at once. They hurried to the waterfront, and went nearly all the way back to the hotel walking through the surf. It was lots of fun.

Suddenly Nan's toe hit something hard. "Ouch!" she exclaimed.

"What's the matter?" Bert asked.

Instead of answering, Nan leaned down and picked something out of the water. Holding it up, she cried out excitedly:

"I've found a treasure!"

CHAPTER XXI

A RIDE IN THE SKY

THERE was no mistaking the fact that Nan Bobbsey had found a treasure. In her hands was a piece of driftwood, filled with shiny pieces of something which looked like pearls.

"What do you suppose it is?" Nan asked her twin.

Bert shrugged. Then he suggested that they show it to Miss Windy. When Nan agreed, the twins hurried towards the curio shop as fast as they could. Bert's ankle was beginning to feel tired and sore, but in the excitement he almost forgot this.

Just before reaching the shop, they saw Mrs. Bobbsey coming up the beach with Freddie and Flossie. The small twins had tired of playing in the sand because Freddie's cave had fallen in, so they had asked their mother to walk up the beach to meet Bert and Nan.

"What have you there?" Freddie called out, seeing the large, queer-shaped thing that Nan held.

"We don't know yet," she replied. "It's a driftwood treasure I found in the water. We were just going to ask Miss Windy about it," she added, displaying the beautiful, pearl-like circular pieces which were embedded in the driftwood.

"That looks like mother-of-pearl," said Mrs. Bobbsey.

"Are they oysters?" asked Flossie, who had once found a pearl in an oyster shell.

Mrs. Bobbsey smiled, saying mother-of-pearl was the inside of the oyster or other shells.

"So maybe it's the driftwood's grandmother," Bert said. He winked, and Flossie laughed.

"I can't understand how the mother-of-pearl stayed in the wood," said Mrs. Bobbsey. "I should think the water would have soaked it out long ago."

When they reached Miss Windy's shop, the old lady was as excited as the children about Nan's find. She said she too thought it was mother-of-pearl. The piece of driftwood evidently had been part of a large treasure box. No doubt jewellery or rare perfumes had been kept in it.

Mrs. Bobbsey asked Miss Windy how the pieces of mother-of-pearl had managed to stay in the wood and not be soaked out.

"My guess is," she answered, "that the box was kept inside a safe or some other container. Probably the ship it was on was wrecked and the safe went to the bottom of the sea." She laughed. "But don't ask me how this piece of the box got to the surface."

"Maybe a big whale ran into it and broke the safe open," Freddie suggested.

The others laughed and said Freddie's guess was as good as anybody else's. Hearing this, Flossie decided to make a guess too.

"Maybe a great big swordfish ran his sword right through the safe," she giggled.

Bert said perhaps the chest belonged to a pirate. He had heard about ships being sunk by pirates so that they could take away all the money and valuable things on board.

"It's too bad we didn't find the whole box," he said. "It might have had a lot of valuable things in it for you to sell, Miss Windy."

In the excitement Miss Windy had not realized that the twins had brought this for her to sell. She had assumed that they expected to take it home. Smiling, she said:

"You children found this curio. Don't you think you ought to take it home and not leave it here?"

Nan, who always wanted to help people, said, "No, Miss Windy, it's for you. We had a lovely ride with your brother, and we'd like to do this for you."

So the curio-shop lady accepted the strange, mysterious piece of driftwood with the mother-of-pearl trimming. Just as the Bobbseys were leaving, a man came in looking for an unusual birthday gift for his wife. Spying the treasure Nan had found, he exclaimed:

"Just what I want!"

The Bobbseys hurried away, glad that Miss Windy was making a nice sale. They did not know how much she was going to charge for the valuable piece of driftwood, but they were sure it would be a good bit of money.

On the way back to the hotel, the older twins told of their long walk up the beach and their failure to find Drifty's cabin.

"But we think we may know where he lives," Bert said. "An old lady told us."

Mrs. Bobbsey was about to say that perhaps the police should help find the man, when all thoughts of Drifty went away from their minds. Who should come walking up the beach towards them but Mr. Bobbsey!

"Dad!" shrieked Flossie, and ran as hard as she could, to swing into her father's arms.

"Why, Fat Fairy, how are you?" Mr. Bobbsey said. He often called Flossie his Fat Fairy. "And Freddie my little Fireman, how've you been?"

"I'm fine, Daddy," Freddy replied, "but I'm not a fireman now. I'm a detective, only I haven't found the *Challenger* yet."

Mrs. Bobbsey kissed her husband, then said that Freddie had also played another game while his father was gone. He was a guide on Captain Windy's clipper ship. When Mr. Bobbsey heard the story, he laughed. But he said it was a good thing he was not at home, or he would have been worried about Freddie's absence too.

"Have you finished all the business you went to attend to?" Mrs. Bobbsey asked.

"No, my dear, I haven't," her husband replied. "But it won't take me long to finish it. I'll be back in time for the big race. How are things coming, Bert?"

His son told him that the *Rover* was registered and that Mr. Ketch had said it was very speedy.

"That's fine, son," Mr. Bobbsey said, patting Bert on the shoulder. "Well, I have a surprise for my family," he added.

"What is it?" all four twins asked together.

Their father said that a pilot friend of his was coming there with a seaplane. He would be glad to take them all for a ride over Whitesail Harbour if they would like to go.

"Oh, that'll be fine!" Bert exclaimed.

"What's a seaplane?" Flossie asked.

Before her father could reply, Freddie told her that it was an aeroplane that could walk on the water like a bird. The others laughed, and said Freddie was partly right, but that a seaplane did not have legs.

"Anyway," Freddie said, "It goes up real high like a bird, and it can swoop down on the water just like those little birds you can see out on the ocean."

All of them were eager to make the flight, and Mr. Bobbsey said the aviator would be there the next morning.

All of them were up early next day, and as soon

as they had finished breakfast, they walked up the beach to where the seaplane was going to land. About ten o'clock a plane swooped down from the sky.

"I see it!" Freddie shouted. "It's landing!"

In a few minutes, the pilot, whose name was Mr. Jackson, taxied the plane up to a large pier, stepped out and met the Bobbsey family. He suggested that they take turns going up. First he would take Mr. Bobbsey and the small twins. When he got back he would take Bert and Nan and their mother.

"That will be thrilling," Mrs. Bobbsey said.

Bert and Nan said nothing, but they were a little envious of their small brother and sister going up first. They stood on the sand, watching the seaplane take off, circle around, and head out across the water.

"He's doing a trick!" Nan cried, as the plane made a dive towards the water.

For a few seconds Mrs. Bobbsey was worried. But the pilot pulled the seaplane up, soared high, and presently it was out of sight.

The small twins had a wonderful time, looking way down below. When they got far out over the water, the pilot pointed and said:

"See? There's a sailing boat race going on down below us. If you watch you can see which one comes in first. They have to go around those markers, and the first one that comes near the shore will win."

Freddie and Flossie kept their noses tight against

the glass of the seaplane's windows. Freddie declared that the boats were not real—they must be toys, they looked so small.

"They're real all right!" his father said. "Look at that one go!"

There was one sleek boat which soon pulled ahead of all the others. It went around the course in fast time, and even though the chidren were high, high above the contest, they knew without a doubt who the winner was.

Ten minutes later Mr. Jackson put his plane into a long glide, and landed beside the pier. When Mr. Bobbsey and the small twins stepped out, Mrs. Bobbsey, Bert, and Nan got into the seaplane. This time the pilot went up a little faster than he had before. His passengers were thrilled, looking down on the water. Very soon the shoreline disappeared.

"Are we going out of sight of land?" Bert asked excitedly.

The pilot nodded, saying he thought the twins would think this was fun. On the way back, Nan suddenly had an idea. "Mr. Jackson," she said, "would you mind going home a special way?"

The pilot said he would not mind a bit, provided it did not take him too far out of his way. Nan assured him that it would not.

"We're trying to find an old beachcomber named Drifty," she said. "We think we know where his hut is, but if we can locate it from the air, it'll be much easier to find out after we land."

Mr. Jackson said he would be very glad to fly

home right along the edge of the beach, so they might look down and hunt for the cabin. On the way back he turned to the left, and as they reached the shore, he flew parallel to it. They had not gone far, when suddenly Bert exclaimed:

"I think I see something written in the sand!"

By this time the pilot had gone beyond the spot, so he turned around and went back over it. Sure enough, in very large letters that had been scrawled in the sand was the word: H-E-L-P.

CHAPTER XXII

THE SCARY BIRD

"SOMEBODY'S in trouble down there!" Nan exclaimed.

"And spelled out HELP in the sand so an aeroplane could see it!" Bert put in excitedly.

"It surely looks that way," Mr. Jackson agreed. "I'll take my plane down near the sign, and see if we can find out who made it."

The pilot landed his plane on a small river which ran into the bay. After taxiing up to a rickety, abandoned fisherman's wharf, he opened the door of the seaplane.

They all stepped out and hurried through the sand and bushes until they came to the spot where they had seen the HELP sign. Nestled among some low trees near by was a hut, its door half open. As the Bobbseys walked over to it and peered inside, they were startled by a man's voice.

"Come in folks! Come in! I suppose you saw my sign for help. I thought nobody was ever going to."

The Bobbseys could see a thin old man lying on a couch. He did not get up.

"Are you Drifty?" Nan asked, before her mother could speak to the man.

"Yes, I am," he answered. "I fell and hurt my back, and I can't walk."

"Oh, I'm so sorry," Mrs. Bobbsey said. "I'm

glad we found you. We'll see that you get to a hospital."

"Thank you, ma'am," Drifty replied, "but I don't see how you can get me out of here. It's a long way to a road and my back hurts so, I can't help myself."

Mr. Jackson told the old beachcomber that his seaplane was not far away. They would fly him to the airport, and from there he could go in an ambulance to the hospital. Drifty frowned as if he did not understand.

"A seaplane?" he asked. "Is that what I heard you say?"

The others nodded, and explained how they had come.

"Well, I've never been in a plane," Drifty said, "but I can't stand this pain in my back any longer, so I guess I'll have to go the way you say."

Quickly Bert and the pilot set to work, making a stretcher out of a blanket and two oars they found in a corner of the hut. Then the four gently lifted Drifty on to the stretcher. With Mrs. Bobbsey and Bert at one end, and Mr. Jackson and Nan at the other, they carried the injured man to the seaplane.

After they had placed Drifty carefully on the floor inside the plane, the pilot took off, and in a short time was circling over the airport just outside Whitesail Harbour.

"This plane can land on either sea or earth, can't it?" Nan asked.

The pilot said yes—as a matter of fact, it could land almost anywhere. And then, with twinkling eyes, he added:

"If the roof of the hospital were only flat, I'd even try landing on it."

The twins smiled, wondering whether the pilot was fooling. They had no chance to find out, because at this moment the plane landed. The Bobbseys discovered that while they had been busy trying to make Drifty comfortable, Mr. Jackson had radioed the airport to call an ambulance. Now it drove up.

Before Drifty was lifted out, he thanked his rescuers. Then he looked at Bert.

"Son," he said, "will you do me a favour? I work for Miss Windy, who runs the curio shop. Tell her I didn't mean to fall down on the job of bringing her treasures from the beach. Ask her please to hold my job open. I'll be well in a short time after those doctor fellows fix me up."

Bert promised to deliver the message, and Nan told the beachcomber that they knew Miss Windy, and had already been helping her. They would continue as long as they stayed at Whitesail Harbour.

"I hope you'll be well by the time we go home," Mrs. Bobbsey said, as the old man was lifted from the plane to the ambulance.

After he had been driven away, Mr. Jackson flew Mrs. Bobbsey and the twins back to the dock where they had boarded his craft. As they alighted, Mr. Bobbsey and the small twins wanted to know what had been going on. They had watched the seaplane go right overhead and come down on land some distance away.

"It was very exciting," Nan said, and told them how they had rescued Windy after spotting the HELP sign in the sand.

Freddie looked hurt. When Nan asked him what was the matter, he said, "I'm the detective. I should have found Drifty."

The others laughed, saying Freddie could be a detective another way. Mrs. Bobbsey told him that they were all going to help Miss Windy by finding treasures on the beach until Drifty was able to work again.

The next morning, after Mr. Bobbsey had left on business, the small twins asked permission to go on the beach and hunt for treasures. Mrs. Bobbsey was willing, but made them promise not to go into the water. They had not been hunting very long before Flossie cried out that she had found something "be-yootiful!"

"What is it?" Freddie called.

"You come and look," Flossie answered. "It's a wonderful shell!"

Her twin hurried over. Seeing the shell, he declared they should go at once to Miss Windy's shop and give it to her. He felt a little sorry that he had not found one like it.

When they handed her the shell, she looked it over carefully and said, "I have never seen one like this. It's so large and beautiful. I believe that the little animal who lived in it didn't inhabit these waters."

"Then how did the shell get here?" Freddie asked.

Miss Windy said she had an idea it might have been brought on a ship, and then dropped overboard.

"Maybe it came on Captain Windy's ship," Flossie suggested.

Miss Windy shook her head, saying the captain never carried shells on his ship. No, she was more inclined to think that it had come on some ship which had been wrecked.

"Then it's all right for you to keep it?" Flossie asked. "And sell it, and give some of the money away?"

"Yes, it's all right for me to do that if I want to," the shop owner answered. "Why did you ask"

"'Cause Drifty needs the money, and a seaplane took him to the hospital."

Poor Flossie was so mixed up that Miss Windy had to ask her to start all over again and tell her what she meant.

Flossie did better the second time and told how Drifty had been found and was now in the hospital. He was coming back to work as soon as he could. In the meantime, Freddie and Flossie and the other Bobbseys were going to find treasures for the curio shop.

"Why, that's very sweet and kind of you," said Miss Windy. "And I think it's wonderful Drifty was rescued."

"Well, good-bye," said Freddie suddenly. "I have to go and find a treasure, too."

With that he raced out of the door, Flossie at his heels. The children hunted for a long time before finding anything more. Freddie was just becoming discouraged, when he noticed strange footprints in the sand.

"They belong to some kind of bird with big feet," he said. "Flossie, let's track it down!"

The twins walked along the edge of the water,

following the bird's footprints. Presently the marks turned up the beach and went into a little grove of trees.

"Maybe we'd better be careful," Flossie suggested. "If it's a great big bird, it might hurt us."

Freddie paid no attention to her advice. He was sure that if there had been any bird around, it would have made itself known by this time. He kept walking to see if perhaps he could find the bird's nest.

"I see it!" he cried a moment later.

"You see what?" Flossie asked.

"The bird's nest," Freddie answered. "And it's a treasure nest!" he exclaimed. "It's full of pretty eggs."

The little boy had hardly finished speaking when there was a terrific squawking behind the children Frightened, they whirled around to see what it was.

CHAPTER XXIII

A MYSTERIOUS BOX

"OOO-EEE!" Flossie cried, and hugged Freddie tightly.

In front of them stood a tall bird with long legs and a hooked beak. It looked very fierce, but to the children's relief it did not come any closer to them. A moment later it flapped its great wings and took off into the sky.

"I'm glad he's gone," said Flossie, and added, "Do you suppose that bird lives in this nest?"

Freddie considered. Then he said he did not think the nest was big enough for the bird, and he asked Flossie to help him lift it down. When they examined the eggs closely, they found that the ends of them were broken.

"Oh, the baby birds are gone!" Flossie cried.

"That was a long time ago, I guess," said Freddie.

Playing detective, he decided that the bird's footprints that they had followed could not have belonged to the bird which had lived in the nest. Nevertheless, he decided the nest and its eggs were worth taking to Miss Windy.

When they walked into her curio shop, Miss Windy smiled. She said the twins certainly were working hard for her, and she appreciated it. The nest and the eggs, she told them, were rare in this part of the country.

"I've heard of certain parrot-like hawks coming here in the spring, building nests and laying eggs. But later the birds leave, and one rarely sees them. I myself have never seen their eggs—only pictures of them."

"Are you glad to have these?" Freddie asked. He could not wait another second to find out.

"Indeed I am," Miss Windy replied, "and I'll certainly be able to sell the nest and eggs easily."

After thanking them, she told the twins that Mrs. Bobbsey had telephoned, asking if Flossie and Freddie were there. They had gone out of sight, and she was a bit worried.

"You'd better return to the hotel at once," Miss Windy suggested.

"All right," said Flossie. "Come on, Freddie."

When they reached the hotel, they found Mrs. Bobbsey and the older twins talking about a letter Bert had just received from Mr. Warren.

"What does it say?" Flossie asked.

Bert told her that the teacher had heard nothing about his missing midget motorboat. He was afraid the *Challenger* was lost forever.

"That certainly is a shame," Mrs. Bobbsey remarked. "I can't imagine anybody being so mean as to take a prize boat."

"Mr. Warren thinks I ought to go to Captain Windy," Bert continued, "and talk to him about wind and weather conditions at Whitesail Harbour. He says it's important to know this for the race."

"Please take me with you when you go to see Captain Windy," Freddie begged.

"Me too," said Flossie.

After lunch all the children went to call on the captain, who was busy showing people around the clipper ship. When he saw Freddie, the skipper asked him to stand by the porpoise tank and tell the story of how he had fallen in. Freddie was pleased. Standing up very straight, he told the story well, and all the crowd laughed.

After the group of sightseers had left the clipper, Bert told the captain about his letter from Mr. Warren.

"Too bad about that motorboat of his," Captain Windy said.

"Yes," Bert answered, and asked, "Could you find a little time to help me with the *Rover?* I want to try it out on the course tomorrow."

Captain Windy said he would be glad to take off a little time to help Bert, but that actually it should have been Drifty.

"That beachcomber is a whiz," he said. "All he has to do is put his nose down to the bay, and he can tell you exactly what the weather is going to be for a week to come!"

The children laughed. They had often heard about tall sea stories, and they were sure this was one of Captain Windy's. But there was probably some truth in it, and Bert hoped that the poor old beachcomber would be well enough to see the race and perhaps give him some good advice about the wind.

Next day the captain met Bert and Freddie at the spot where the race would take place. Markers had been put in the water to show the course. Freddie asked Captain Windy a hundred questions about the contest.

"It's an exciting one," the captain answered. "I've seen it several years in a row. The boats are fast, and you'll have a hard time winning, Bert."

As the boy set his boat in the water, Freddie said, "How are you going to get the *Rover* back when it gets way out in the harbour?"

Captain Windy said they would hire a rowing boat to do this.

"Please, may I row?" Freddie asked.

The captain said he might take one oar, perhaps. It would be too difficult for the little boy to row three persons in the type of rowing boat which they would use.

While Captain Windy went to get the boat, Bert tinkered with the *Rover*. He turned this, pulled that, and mystified his small brother completely.

"Why don't you leave it alone?" Freddie asked finally. "You won two races in Lakeport. Maybe you'll spoil the *Rover*."

Bert said that he was merely trying to increase the speed. Also, he was trying to adjust the rudder so that the little boat would go straight, even though there were tiny waves in the harbour.

"And what about the wind?" his brother wanted to know.

Bert had to admit that he knew nothing about this. He would have to wait until Captain Windy returned and told him how to adjust the rudder.

Presently the elderly man arrived with the rowing boat, and the two boys climbed in. Freddie seated himself beside the captain and took one of the oars. He soon found it was very hard work and gave up. He moved to the prow of the boat and looked around.

"Here come some other people with midget boats," he announced presently.

Three other rowing boats could be seen, the people in them holding midget speedboats on their laps. One by one the boats were put into the water. Bert watched them speed away.

"Boy, can they go!" he exclaimed. "I wonder how the *Rover* will do."

Captain Windy put his face into the wind. Then having decided how strong the wind was, he moved the rudder on Bert's boat a little.

"Now, try it out," he suggested.

Bert started the motor, and set his boat in the

course. It went straight as an arrow for some distance, then suddenly it began to turn.

"Oh, it's going to hit the marker!" Freddie shouted.

Fortunately the *Rover* missed the marker, but Bert knew that he would have to change the position of the rudder. They rowed across the water and rescued the little boat. Then work began on the test in earnest, and it was a whole hour before Captain Windy and Bert were satisfied with their progress.

All this time Nan and Flossie had been walking up and down the beach searching for curios for Miss Windy's shop. They had had no luck.

Both girls were getting such a sunburn that Nan suggested they walk under a pier just ahead and get out of the heat a while. Flossie was glad to do this, and skipped ahead of her sister. When the two girls found a cool spot, they sat down to rest.

"It's a shame we haven't found anything," said Flossie. "What will poor Miss Windy do?"

"Oh, maybe something will turn up," Nan said hopefully. "We'll look again this afternoon. After all, Miss Windy still has a lot of things to sell."

Flossie let her eyes wander up to the underside of the pier. She was intrigued at all the sea life attached to it. There were barnacles and pieces of seaweed, as well as thousands of tiny shells.

Suddenly her eyes spied a little box which had been jammed back in a corner. Jumping up, she tried to reach it. Unable to, she pointed the spot out to Nan, and asked her to lift the little box down.

Even Nan could not reach it. She wondered about trying to climb one of the poles but they were very slippery.

"Maybe I can jump up and hold on to one of the beams," she thought, "and grab the box."

It took three tries before she was able to do this, but finally Nan did knock the box from its hiding place. As it fell to the sand, the lid came off.

"Why, it's full of alphabets!" Flossie said. "They're nice shiny letters. Maybe they belong to a school."

Nan laughed. "If those brass letters belong to a school, it must be a school of fishes," she said. More seriously, she added that it was strange that the letters should be hidden under the pier.

Nan sat down and looked more closely at them. They were about half an inch high and looked as if they had been ripped from something.

"What do they spell?" Flossie asked.

Nan had no idea, but she began to arrange the letters in various groups. At first she could figure nothing out of them. Then she got the words "call her," but an *e*, *n*, and *g* were left over. Finally these letters gave Nan an idea. Quickly she rearranged all of them. Then excitedly she exclaimed:

"Flossie, those little letters spell *Challenger!*"

CHAPTER XXIV

DANNY'S SECRET

"WE'VE found the *Challenger!*" Flossie cried, after she and Nan had raced back to the hotel. "I mean we found the letters."

Quickly Nan explained to her brother about the box of letters which spelled *Challenger*.

"I'm sure they must belong to Mr. Warren's boat," she said.

Her twin was sure they did, too. The children spoke to Mrs. Bobbsey, who advised Bert to take the letters at once to the racing headquarters.

"I believe that the person who has the *Challenger* brought it here to put in the race," she said.

"And took off the letters," Nan added.

"He probably painted another name on the boat," said Bert.

He hurried to the racing office, and fortunately found Mr. Ketch, the pleasant official to whom he had talked before.

The boy was careful not to accuse anyone, but

171

told the story of the missing *Challenger* from beginning to end. Then he took the little box from his pocket and laid the letters on the man's desk.

"Did anyone enter a boat that looks like the *Challenger?*" Bert asked, and described Mr. Warren's boat as best he could.

Mr. Ketch said he was not certain. He took a book on boats from a shelf and looked through the index. In a moment he turned to a page near the back and pointed out a picture to Bert.

"There's the *Challenger,*" he said, "with Mr. Warren's name under it. If that's the boat you mean, a man did bring one in here which has lines very much like it."

"That's the one," said Bert.

The official looked grave, saying this was a very shocking situation. He would look through the applications of the contestants to see if everything was in order, and would let Bert know the results.

The boy left Mr. Ketch's office, wondering what would happen. The next day the official telephoned him at the hotel, asking if Bert would come over immediately.

"Yes, sir. Right away." Bert promised.

When he got there, Bert noticed that several boats were standing on a shelf. Mr. Ketch explained that he had asked the owners to bring them to his office to be looked over before the race. Would Bert examine them carefully and see if one might be the missing *Challenger?*

"I can tell you right now," Bert said, pointing

to one called the *Eagle*. "That looks exactly like Mr. Warren's stolen boat."

Mr. Ketch said again that this was a very serious charge. He would have to be absolutely sure about the boat before accusing the man who had entered it.

"Do you think you could find any identifying mark on it, Bert, to be positive you aren't making a mistake?" he asked.

Bert took the boat from the shelf and turned it round and round. He peered inside, then looked at the bottom of it. He could find no special marks which he remembered.

He was about to tell this to Mr. Ketch, when something caught his eye. It was a tiny hole near the letter *g* of the word *Eagle*.

"Mr. Ketch," Bert said excitedly, "maybe this hole is where one of the *Challenger* letters was ripped off! May I scrape off a tiny bit of the varnish where the other letters might have been?"

Mr. Ketch said that under the circumstances he thought it was all right. In a few minutes Bert had proved his point. The brass letters spelling *Challenger* had most definitely been taken off the boat now named the *Eagle*!

"That was very clever," Mr. Ketch praised Bert. He reached for the telephone and put in two calls. One was to a Mr. Wall, who had entered the *Eagle*; the other to police headquarters. Hanging up, Mr. Ketch asked if Bert would please wait.

"A plain-clothes man will stand outside the

door and listen to what Mr. Wall has to say," he told Bert.

A few minutes later Mr. Wall arrived. He was a large, red-faced man, who said he had no time to waste. What did Mr. Ketch want?

Bert admired the smooth way the official got around to accusing the man of stealing the *Challenger*, removing the letters, and changing the name. Mr. Walls blustered, denied everything, and finally made a dash for the door. But the plain-clothes man grabbed him and brought him back inside the office.

"Now tell us the truth," the policeman said sternly.

Thoroughly frightened, Mr. Wall said, "There's not much to it. I wanted to race a good motor-boat, and I couldn't afford to buy one. Say," he added, suddenly pointing at Bert, "who's this kid? Get him out of here."

"No, he's staying," said Mr. Ketch. "This is Bert Bobbsey, and he gets all the credit for solving this mystery."

Bert in turn said that actually his two sisters had found the letters, which helped to solve the case.

"When did you take the *Challenger* from the recreation building on Lake Metoka?" Bert asked the man.

Mr. Wall said that he had not actually taken it himself. He had asked a boy he knew in Lake-port to help him. Mr. Wall admitted he had lied to the boy, telling him that Mr. Warren had lent him the boat. He had asked the boy to go to Mr. Warren's classroom and pick it up.

"Was it——?" Bert started to say "Danny Rugg," then changed his mind.

Even if it were Danny, the boy was innocent. Bert was sorry now that he had ever thought him guilty of stealing the boat. He wondered, though, if he would ever find out if it were Danny. In a few minutes Mr. Ketch told Bert that he might leave, and wished him luck in the race.

When Bert reached the hotel, the first person he met was Ken Strong. The boy had come to have dinner with his parents. As soon as Bert had said hello to him, Ken exclaimed:

"I found out about Danny Rugg for you! He did bring a boat to camp and it was named the *Challenger*. But a man came the next day and took it away."

Bert burst out laughing. Then he explained to Ken that he had solved the last link in the mystery. Just then Nan and the rest of the family came up. Bert told them the whole story.

"Well, I'm glad Danny is not really a thief," Nan remarked. "But he's an awfully mean boy just the same."

"Say, Danny's A W O L from camp," Ken told them.

Freddie and Flossie looked puzzled and asked what this meant. Ken explained that the initials stood for *absent without official leave*.

"Do you suppose Danny knows we found out about the *Challenger*?" Bert asked.

Ken shrugged, saying the fellows at camp thought Danny had sneaked away to look over the boats which would race. He had asked permission to go, but this had not been granted, because he had played a mean trick at camp.

"The race is tomorrow, isn't it?" Ken asked. "A lot of us boys are coming. We wouldn't miss it for anything."

The Bobbseys were glad the mystery was solved, and now looked forward eagerly to the big race. Early next morning Captain Windy arrived at the hotel. To Bert's surprise he had Drifty with him.

"I just had to get well so I could see the race." The old beachcomber grinned. "I understand the captain here wants me to tell you something about the wind."

"That's right," Bert said. "Let's go down to the course right away and set the *Rover*'s rudder."

The three started off, but they had gone only a few steps when they found Freddie tagging along. The little boy remarked that he wanted to see Drifty lay his nose on the water.

The old beachcomber looked amazed, and wanted to know what Freddie meant. Bert laughed and said that evidently his brother had heard him repeat a phrase Captain Windy had said. It was:

"When Drifty lays his nose to the bay, he can tell you what the weather's going to be for two weeks ahead."

Drifty laughed heartily, and said Captain Windy had exaggerated slightly. He would be very glad to put his face down near the water, however, and see just what the wind was.

"Most folks don't realize," he said, "that the wind right down by the water isn't the same as it is a few feet in the air."

Bert said he had never heard this, and certainly appreciated Drifty's helping him set the rudder right, so the *Rover* would stay on course.

"Wind's east by nor'east," the beachcomber announced a few moments later.

Again and again the rudder was moved and tried out in the water. Finally they had it exactly right to keep the *Rover* from being blown off the course by the "east by nor'east wind".

Noticing that Bert was getting jittery, Captain Windy suggested that the boy forget about the race for a few hours, and take a little trip with him.

"On the clipper?" Bert asked.

The skipper said no, he thought it would be more restful if he hired a rowing boat and took Freddie and Bert out to Lonely Island. The children had not heard of the little uninhabited island out in the bay, and were eager to go.

It took about three-quarters of an hour to row out to Lonely Island. They pulled the boat up on the beach among the trees and set off to the far side.

Presently Captain Windy pulled some sand-wiches from his pocket, and suggested they sit down and eat. He told several interesting stories, and then looking at his watch, said:

"I guess we'd better start back now."

"Yes," Bert agreed. "I want to ask Drifty about the wind at the very last minute before the race. The rudder might have to be adjusted again."

The three of them crossed the little island, coming back to the spot where they had left the rowing boat. Freddie was in the lead. Suddenly the others heard him shout:

"Our boat's gone!"

Captain Windy and Bert rushed to the beach. Freddie was right. There was no sign of the rowing boat. Worse than that, there was no sign of any other boat within hailing distance.

Bert's face became pale. Suppose he was not able to get back in time for the race!

CHAPTER XXV

A BIG VICTORY

"WE must get back, Captain Windy," Bert said, when he found his voice.

The worried boy was trembling, and Freddie felt like crying. The captain's face was very sober.

"A boat ought to come along pretty soon," Captain Windy said hopefully. "We'll keep our eyes open."

But none did and finally he suggested that the boys stay there, while he looked on the other side of the island.

As he left, Bert's hopes sank. He had glanced at Captain Windy's wrist-watch, and had seen that it was already one o'clock. The race began at two. Even if a boat should come along, they might not get back in time!

"I'll climb a tree and wave," Freddie offered. He could think of nothing else to do. But when he saw that the trees were small and gnarled, he gave up the idea.

Suddenly Bert cried:

"I think I hear the *putt-putt* of a motor!"

"I see it! I see it!" Freddie cried gleefully, "There's a boat heading for the other side of the island!"

As the brothers raced among the trees, they heard Captain Windy shouting to them. Running faster, they soon came to his side.

Nearing the shore was a good-sized motorboat!

"Are you folks shipwrecked, captain?" the pilot asked. He came as close as he dared without running into the sand.

"Worse than that, skipper," Captain Windy called to the man, whom he had known for a long time. "Can you take us to Whitesail Harbour?"

"I sure can. Is there something the matter?"

Bert spoke up, saying he wanted to go into the midget speedboat race, and there was very little time left. Someone had stolen their rowing boat, and they were marooned on the island.

While he was talking, the boy was splashing through the water towards the motorboat. Captain Windy picked Freddie up in his arms, and followed. The three climbed into the motorboat, which set off for the Whitesail Harbour pier at a good clip.

Bert glanced again at Captain Windy's wristwatch. It was one-thirty!

"How long will it take us, skipper?" he asked the pilot.

"About fifteen minutes."

This would make it quarter to two, Bert figured. Only fifteen minutes would be left for him to go all the way to the hotel, pick up his boat, and get to the race.

With a sinking heart, Bert felt that he never could make it in time. He sat very still, not saying another word until they reached the pier. Then he quickly thanked the pilot, and jumped out.

To his amazement there on the pier stood Drifty. And in Drifty's arms was the *Rover*!

"Oh, Drifty, you've saved the day!" Bert cried.

"I thought you might need me," the beach-comber said with a wink.

Captain Windy hailed a taxi, and the four of them climbed in. They drove as near to the course as they could, and then hurried down through the sand. It was five minutes to two when Bert reported!

"Now, Bert, don't you worry one speck," Drifty told him. "I've been keeping track of the wind on the water. It hasn't changed a bit since this morning. You just leave that rudder the way it is, and I'm sure the little *Rover* will do you credit."

Just then Nan and Flossie ran up to the boys.

"Daddy's here!" Flossie exclaimed. "And guess who else!"

Bert turned around to see his parents, and—Mr. Warren! The teacher grinned and shook the boy's hand.

"Good work, Bert," he said. "Mr. Ketch telephoned me about your finding my boat. I hurried here to thank you, and watch the big race. Good luck!"

Before Bert could say anything, a clock boomed out. It was two o'clock! The zero hour for Bert Bobbsey!

All the contestants' boats were quickly lined up. The positions had been allotted by the racing officials, and the *Rover* was exactly in the centre.

A pistol shot rang out and away went all the midget speedboats. The spectators cheered. But they became quiet as they watched first one boat, then another take the lead. Within a few minutes several of the boats had veered off the course, and were declared out of the race. Their rudders had not been set right.

"The *Rover's* still in!" Freddie shouted.

Five boats were now about even, with the *Rover* still in the centre of the course. A man near Bert remarked that he had never seen a boat go straighter down a course than the one in the middle.

"That's my brother's boat!" Freddie said proudly. "And he made it himself."

Suddenly the two boats on the outside angled off, one to the left, the other to the right. They were out of the race!

This left only three, with the *Rover* still in the middle. Presently Bert's and the one to the left, the *Red Wing,* pulled ahead.

"Oh!" Oh!" Flossie suddenly screamed. "That bad boat hit Bert's."

The *Red Wing* had turned towards the *Rover* and bumped smack into the side of it. In a few seconds it would push the *Rover* off course!

Then, when they were only five yards from the finish line, the *Red Wing* lost speed and dropped far behind.

The third boat, now only two yards behind, was speeding straight towards its goal. If the *Rover* could not stay within bounds, the other one would win.

Presently, from a motorboat far out in the water, Mr. Ketch signalled that the race was over. There was silence while everyone waited to hear the announcement.

Bert's heart was thumping so hard that he could hardly breathe. Flossie had her hands over her ears. She was afraid to listen

"Ladies and gentlemen," came Mr. Ketch's voice through a megaphone, "the winner—by a hair's breadth—is the *Rover,* owned by Bert Bobbsey!"

"Oh, my boat did it!" Bert cried out, as the clapping started.

Freddie jumped on Bert's back, and Nan and Flossie kissed him. Then Mr. and Mrs. Bobbsey gave their son a hug, and Mr. Warren slapped him on the shoulder.

At this moment Ken Strong came running up. After congratulating Bert, he asked what had made him so late getting to the race.

"Boy, you had me scared," he said.

When Bert told him the reason, Ken shouted, "I know who the pirate was!"

"Pirate?" Freddie asked, his eyes popping.

"Yes. It was Danny Rugg," Ken replied. "He was so mad when you found out about the *Challenger* that he wanted to get square. He saw you start out for Lonely Island, so he helped himself to the camp motorboat to follow you and take the rowing boat. A supervisor saw him coming back and reported him. He's going to be punished."

Suddenly all the spectators roared with laughter. Captain Windy, Drifty, and Mr. Warren were doing a few steps from the Sailor's Hornpipe.

"Everybody's so happy you won, Bert," said Mrs. Bobbsey.

By this time, Mr. Ketch had retrieved the midget boats and brought the *Rover* back to Bert.

"The champion of Whitesail Harbour," he said proudly, as he put the boat in the boy's arms.

Then he presented Bert with the trophy of the race, a beautiful silver cup. All the spectators clapped and cheered, but the Bobbseys cheered Bert loudest of all.

Read more of the Twins' adventures in
"THE BOBBSEY TWINS AT MYSTERY MANSION"